Early Praise for *Drifting Too Far From The Shore*

"*Readers will come to love feisty Charlotte "Muddy" Rewis who, despite the bad news in the world, triumphs by making a difference in her own way. Chock full of humor, Drifting Too Far From the Shore is a beautiful story that makes you feel like you have been transported back to small town America.*"

– Winston Groom, author of *Forrest Gump*

"*Drifting Too Far From the Shore marks extraordinary talent. I can't remember the last time that I have enjoyed a book this much. It's beautifully written and compelling, with incredible range. Muddy is richly developed, springing right out of the pages.*"

– Michael Lee West, author of *Crazy Ladies*

DRIFTING TOO FAR FROM THE SHORE

by

Niles Reddick

Summertime Publications

DRIFTING TOO FAR FROM THE SHORE
American paperback edition first published
by Summertime Publications Inc (USA) in 2016

cover design by Vanessa Mendozzi
photo by Francisco Rangel

Library of Congress Cataloging-in-Publication Data
Reddick, Niles
Drifting Too Far From The Shore / Niles Reddick 1st edition
Library of Congress Control Number: 2015960812

Summertime Publications Inc.
4115 East Palo Verde Drive, Phoenix, AZ 85018
All Rights Reserved
ISBN 978-1-940333-09-0

for Earl

Table of Contents

Drifting too far from the Shore

Inspired by

"Drifting too far from the Shore"

by Charles Ernest Moody of the Georgia Yellow Hammers 1924,

as performed by Dolly Parton and Porter Wagoner

Why meet a terrible fate

Mercies abundantly wait

Turn back before it's too late

You're drifting too far from the shore

Chapter 1

In memory of Mary Turner, a 1918 Georgia lynching victim

For Muddy, scenes she relived and imagined in her head were more of a reality than anything on the TV or around her now, but the third doorbell chime in the faux wood box next to the front door brought her back. There had been a couple of times when she almost drifted too far, like the time she drew a bath and laid there soaking and slipped under. That's when she heard Claude's voice whisper, "Muddy." She came to and pushed upward through the suds, coughing and trying to catch her breath, and threw on the terry cloth General Dollar bathrobe one of the grandkids had given her at Christmas. She didn't like the bathrobe as much as she liked the ones she'd bought at Belk's from the lady with a gold capped tooth over in Valdosta, but it was simple and comfortable like a towel or dishrag and it had been a gift.

The other time she almost drifted too far was when she sat in the porch swing, fell asleep, and was awakened by a policeman at 1:00 a.m., having made his rounds with the search light and scanning yards for petty criminals. With a pass of the light, he'd seen something crumpled in the swing, the temperature in the mid-forties that November night. He moved around the azaleas to the clapboard house, thinking one of the homeless might have come out of Valdosta and made his way to Morven, like they'd done before when they normally would escort them two counties over to Echols County, the only place in the state that it was legally acceptable in which to banish people. He'd startled Muddy on the porch with the light in her face, calling, "Ms. Rewis? You okay?"

The voice she heard was Claude's, not the policeman's. "Come on, Muddy."

She had come to a bit and said, "Who's there? Where's Claude? I thought he'd come for me." When the officer explained who he was, she didn't say anything more to mask her confusion. She thanked him, told him she must have fallen asleep, couldn't believe she hadn't gotten cold, got up, and went in. She never told him she thought it was her time, that the light was not his flashlight, but the light in the tunnel. She knew if she had, it would be all over town.

She had reasons for not wanting the story to get out. She didn't care what people thought, but she didn't want anyone in her business, especially her children who would likely come put her in the nursing home or try to get her to move to one of their houses. Two were married, all three were gone, and all three seemed so absorbed in their own lives that they didn't have time for her. That was fine by her. She didn't want to be involved in their lives much now anyway. She'd done all she could do for them, and it didn't mean that she loved them less or that they loved her less; it simply meant she couldn't keep up with it all now, didn't understand their world and ways because it seemed so busy and complicated with computers, the world-wide web, Facebook, i-pods and pads, and so on. She just wanted to move on and see that precious face again, the one that went with the whispers.

As she had aged and family members passed, and particularly since Claude had gone, Muddy had come to believe they were there, just off shore, helping to guide friends and family through nudges and intuitions and even physical acts. She'd come up with this notion after watching an episode of "Touched by an Angel" and recalled instances from her own life, times that were underscored on her brain as being beyond normal. The first time etched in her memory was when she'd gone back to the school to get a book she left behind in third grade and the janitor had cornered her, told her she was pretty, and told her he had something to show her. A gust of wind had come in the opened windows, slamming a closet door, startling him, and drawing his attention away from her, and she'd run out the door. The janitor was arrested later that year for having sex with a cow, being drunk, and lost his job. Of course Muddy didn't know that until she was grown and a classmate had told her at a reunion. Her parents, she figured, had known it, but this was before Donahue and Oprah where everyone discussed anything on TV.

She remembered her bicycle chain breaking just as she was about to cross highway 122 when the light turned green. She was by the curb, straddling the bike with one foot on the pavement and one foot on the pedal with which to push off, and Muddy turned to see the family in the Country Squire station wagon talking and laughing. One of the children was drinking an orange Nehi and another was drinking a Yoo-hoo. She even recalled licking her lips and feeling her stomach grumble. When the light turned green, she pushed down on the right bike pedal, and the chain broke. An eighteen-wheeler hauling chickens ran the red light and broad-sided the Country Squire. The family lived, but they were hurt and had to go to the hospital in Hahira, a town about fifteen miles across the river. Muddy, on the other hand, would have been obliterated, like the birds, squirrels, opossums, and skunks, which were, by far, the worst smelling.

The most recent experience was when Claude died three years ago. She was in the house and felt him, smelled his Bruit cologne, and heard a faint whisper in her ear: "Charlotte." She broke down in the kitchen, dropping tears in cake mix and trying to pull herself together before she called for help and walked to the little barn out back, where he was slumped over the Murray mower from the massive heart attack. Like most of her family and friends in town, Charlotte had been called Muddy since a child when she made mud pies and allegedly had eaten them. Even Claude called her Muddy unless something was terribly wrong.

Her boney fingers, now partly crooked from arthritis with brown spotty skin stretched over, reached in the side pouch and pressed the button that raised the lift chair and she pulled the cane close to her. Most of the time, she could get to the door before too many rings, and if there were people she knew, they knew to wait. If the person was a salesman, then he would move on, probably determining the house wasn't even lived in given the blinds were pulled and the shrubbery that Muddy and Claude would have kept cut back to porch floor level when Claude was alive hadn't been cut in years, some even now pushing on to the edge of the tin roof.

Muddy made it to the door, unlocked the dead bolt, and opened the wooden door. "Hey," she said.

"Hey Mama," Lily said. She stood in a sundress, matching sandals on her feet, matching toe nail polish, matching bag strapped over her shoulder. She pulled the screen door as Muddy made a semi-circle with the cane, heading back to the den to her lift chair, the cane thumping across the heart pine. "Mama, I was about to get worried."

"Don't worry. I ain't dead yet, but hopefully it won't be long."

"Now, Mama, there ain't a thing wrong with you and you know it. You need to get out more, do more, and you'll feel better about life."

"Honey, I been getting out and doing all my life. I'm tired." Muddy eased back in the lift chair. "You want some tea?"

"Not right now. I'll get some in a minute. What about you? Can I get you something?"

"No, I'm fine. Just dozed off in the chair. Wasn't expecting you to come or I would have picked up the place."

"Mama, it looks clean compared to mine," Lily said. "But now, if it's getting to be too much on you, I can get someone to come and clean for you. There's a maid service out of Thomasville that will come over here, and I'll even pay for it. I know how you hate spending your money."

"What money, Lily? Ya'll think I got some money, but I don't. I guess when you get to dividing up all this junk around here, you'll see just how much money I don't have."

"Now, Mama, there ain't no use in getting worked up."

"I ain't worked up."

"Well, you seem worked up."

"I think I know when I'm worked up and not, and I'd think you'd know it, too."

"Okay, then. I was just coming over here to go to the peach shed and get a bushel to put up and thought you might want to ride with me, maybe get you one of them peach ice cream cones."

"Lily, I appreciate it, but I don't care for one. It's got to where dairy is hard on my bowels."

"Well, how about riding down there with me anyway? Just get out of the house for a while."

"I've been going to the peach shed for seventy-something years. I don' think much has changed since last time. You go on. I 'preciate it."

"You want me to get you some peaches?"

"No, the preacher's wife always comes by and brings some when she visits."

"Alright, mama. You been feeling okay?"

"I guess I have. How 'bout you? How're you feeling?"

"Oh, I'm doing alright. Just busy to the point I sometimes don't think I'm able to keep up."

"Why're you so busy?"

"You know the boys are in baseball at the high school and seems like we're either at practice or a game just about every night. Then, with church added in on top of my job at the china shop, it's about too much."

"How's Sid and the boys doing? Boys winning any games? I sure would like to see them play some this year"

"Sid's fine. He's in the woods a lot marking timber or with a crew thinning pines. The boys are fine. Since Todd got him that car, he's gone a lot. Half the time we don't know what he's doing, but we trust him. He has a friend, though, and that worries me."

Muddy knew Lily well enough to know that if she said the word "worry," then she was troubled about something. Of her and Claude's three children, Lily was the most transparent. "What do you mean, Lily?"

"Well, he's gotten a little close to this girl, and well, she's black. Shaneka's her name. I don't think they're dating or nothing, but she goes with him a lot. I don't know what I'd think if he was dating her. We just didn't do that, but today, kids are doing that more and more. She is a sweet girl and has even come to the house to eat some. Her family was from over here somewhere. Their last name's Harris."

"It's a different world today, Lily. I don't know if it's better or worse. Back in my day, there were two lines: the boy/girl line and the black/white line. You just didn't cross it, but things are more even today."

"Yes, it is different. I don't know whether it's better or worse. Did you know the family, mama?"

"There was a woman who cooked in the lunchroom named Harris. Fredonia Harris, I think it was."

"That's got to be her great aunt. She said she had a great aunt who'd been a cook. She also said something about her great grandmother having been killed, and they are supposed to put up a memorial at the Withlacoochee River Bridge. You remember anything about that?"

"Lily, no, it can't be."

"Can't be what?"

"Oh, Lily, I don't think I can tell you about it." Muddy teared and grabbed a Kleenex out of the floral box next to the lift chair and dabbed her eyes. "Lord have mercy, I never wanted to think about that again."

18

"Mama, goodness gracious, what in the world?"

"Back in the 20's, something awful happened. A young black woman named Cassie Harris who was pregnant was lynched. I wasn't even born, but I heard about it at some point and never forgot it."

"Did anyone in your family see it, Mama?"

"Lord, no, but everyone heard about it. It was in the papers and caused riots over in Valdosta. I've often wondered if I might have known some of the people involved, but they are long dead by now. It shouldn't have happened."

"Lord, Mama. I never heard about that before."

"Who would want to hear about it? I think as times changed through the years, you've seen that sort of evil behavior wane, but crimes have been around since the beginning. I think crime always will be because the good Lord gave us free will."

"Maybe so. Well, we should go and support Shaneka and her family at the marker ceremony."

She began to drift and remember the story, shaking her head. "It's a terrible story."

"Tell it," Lily said.

"A plantation owner named Seth Arman had trouble getting people to work for him because he was harsh toward his workers, whether black or white. He began to rely on petty criminals for labor by bailing them out of jail and having them work their debt off at his plantation. One young black man, Fred Harris, had been accused of gambling and put in jail. Once he was at the plantation, still proclaiming innocence, he and Arman got into an argument. Arman shot him. Word spread through town, and Cassie was beside herself. She was enraged, running from home to home banging on doors and demanding justice and claiming she would swear out warrants against the white man, and she was about thirty-two weeks pregnant. No one could comfort her and late that afternoon near dusk, several trucks made their way through town, snatched her from the front yard of her family's home, and took her to the river. Reports were they hung her on a tree limb, dowsed her with gas, burnt her clothes off, slit her belly open, the baby falling to the ground where it was repeatedly stomped, and then both were burned, still alive. Eventually, someone buried the remains by the river." Muddy dabbed her eyes. "You know, Lily, I just don't believe I'd ever heard of such. Later, it came out that Fred Harris was going to make a preacher and had been talking to them men about gambling. It was a shame."

"I'm not sure I know what to say. I've never heard that story before and am not glad to hear it today. Mama, it's almost unreal that something like that could have ever happened."

"I know it. People can be evil." And Muddy wondered about the men who did this to Cassie Harris—if they lived full lives, if they went to church and repented, if their own families knew what they'd done, and she wondered if God forgave such crimes; the insane Jeffrey Dahmers, Ted Bundys, and Charles Mansons of the world. Muddy knew she couldn't and though her Sunday school class would be shocked, she would tell them some of these criminals should be hunted down and killed themselves just like they had done to their innocent victims. She knew two wrongs don't make a right, but letting someone go to jail and sit there, watching TV, going to college through the mail or on the computer, playing games, and getting three good meals a day seemed a major waste of taxpayer dollars, especially when they couldn't raise Social Security for good people who'd worked hard. It disgusted Muddy.

Of course, President Bush had made some positive changes since he'd finally won the election, as Muddy told friends, adding she was glad she didn't live in Florida, not because of the heat and bugs, but because of the dangling chads. She thought it was a shame they hadn't done a better job with elections. At first, she wasn't fond of Bush because he wasn't a good speaker, but he'd supported some prescription drug changes in Medicare Muddy thought were positive and he supported some STEM cell research, which Muddy felt was good for society. She also thought he'd done a good job after September 11th, but she knew, even in Morven, life would never be the same because of crazy terrorists, but they had always been around, just in different forms. She didn't see much of a difference between the men who carried out the World Trade Center plane crashes and the men who murdered Cassie Harris. There was something wrong with them, evil, and it was at their core. Muddy also knew she'd never go in a high building again, even though she hadn't been in any over seven floors and that was at a hotel in Panama City, Florida, nearly twenty years ago.

"I'll go with ya'll," Muddy said. "It's the least I could do."

"I guess I better be getting on. I think they are going to have this marker ceremony right after lunch tomorrow. They're doing it on a Sunday because that's when she died," Lily said.

"Alright, well, I'll be ready to go when ya'll get here," Muddy started the lift chair up.

"No, mama, you just stay there. I'll see myself out."

When Lily went out, the whole story of the brutal killing of Cassie Harris circled in her mind like a flock of birds that keep shifting direction in flight and avoid landing in a tree. She wondered who whispered to Cassie while she was hanging on that tree limb dying. She imagined Cassie's grandmother whispering "Hold on, baby, I'm coming. It won't hurt but a minute." She wondered about the man who doused her with gas, the man who struck the match, the man with the knife who split her belly, the ones who stomped that innocent baby to death. How could they have done something like this to another human being? Did their parents and grandparents raise them that way? Surely, she believed, their grandmothers whispered to them: "Don't you do that. Put that match down. Throw that knife in the river. Don't stomp that child of God." She reckoned that if their people had whispered, they had long dismissed such as nonsense, freely choosing to live life as they saw fit and certainly not playing by anyone's, even God's, rules. Muddy wondered about her own children and grandchildren. She knew she'd be one to help them, guide them.

When Muddy awoke in the lift chair, it was dark outside. She remembered she'd never gone and locked the door after Lily left. She raised the chair, grabbed her cane, locked the door and got to the kitchen where she prepared a tomato sandwich and a glass of tea. She went back to the chair, watched the Grand Ole Opry, a show she loved, especially when Emmylou Harris made an appearance. After the Grand Ole Opry, Muddy watched a rerun of Hee-Haw followed by CNN Headline News for a bit until they recycled stories. Muddy was tired, and she wasn't feeling well. That kerplunk feeling in her chest bothered her a little bit, but she didn't feel any pain when it happened and thought she would mention it soon when she went for her check-up.

The next morning, Muddy piddled around the house, read the newspaper, her Bible, and her daily devotional. She wanted to go to church, but knew she needed her energy for the ceremony and was determined to go, so she stayed home and watched church on TV. She didn't get the full experience, of course, but it served its purpose. She also believed it was good for shut-ins and those who were lost, an outreach or mission effort. Muddy was eating leftover squash casserole and ham for lunch when she heard Lily yell, "Mama."

"In here," Muddy said.

"You ready?" Lily asked.

"I reckon."

"Well, don't you look nice? I like that dress and shoes. Where'd you get them?"

"Over there in Thomasville. You helped me pick them out last year. Don't you remember? You got an outfit, too."

"Lord, I don't even remember."

"Where's Sid and the boys?"

"Sid couldn't come, so he and Tom stayed home. I guess Todd's coming with his friend Shaneka. You know he won't ride with me anymore regardless. They've gone and grown up and are embarrassed by us."

She nodded. Muddy knew that feeling well. Same thing had happened with Lily and her two boys. At some point, they didn't need her as much and it hurt for a while and Muddy realized she had to let them fly and be there when they fell. Muddy wondered about how she might feel if Todd was dating a black girl. She guessed it didn't really matter, but in her day, it wouldn't have been considered acceptable. Muddy thought any sort of interracial relationship would have to be tough and relationships were tough enough without anything extra added on it. From a biblical standpoint, these relationships weren't new. Even Moses had married an African woman and God had sanctioned this marriage.

Lily drove to the site by the Withlacoochee River and several cars had lined up next to the highway. The Department of Transportation hadn't sent the mowing crew alongside Highway 122, so the weeds were almost knee deep in some places. Some of the black seeds from the Bahia grass and sandspurs were getting on Muddy's hose and dress, since the cane knocked them loose as she crept along. There were a few folding chairs someone had put out from a Quitman funeral home, and one of the black men offered Muddy a seat. She took it, and Lily stood behind, waiting to see if another elderly woman or man might need a seat. Muddy was tired, and she'd had two more kerplunks, but didn't mention anything to Lily about it. To her, it felt like the heart stopped and then cranked back up again. She wondered if she didn't have some sort of plaque build-up, just like she got on her teeth over time. She didn't like thinking she might have to have a procedure done on her heart. When Todd and Shaneka arrived, Todd introduced Shaneka to his grandmother. Shaneka smiled, but did not speak, and the two teens moved off, where they stood with some other young people Muddy assumed they knew from school.

A minister from the African Methodist Episcopal church from Quitman offered a prayer, followed by a retelling of the story by the granddaughter of Cassie, Shaneka's mother. It was moving, and Muddy imagined the event--Cassie hanging from the tree not ten feet from where Muddy sat, the baby falling out of the mother's belly and being stomped, the whispers from the grandmothers of the men committing the heinous act. Muddy began to feel the heat from the burning body, and she fanned her face while sweat beads trickled down her back. She heard the screams and cries of torture and the curses, and a face began to form in her mind and she believed it was the devil. She felt another kerplunk and slid right out of the chair and hit the ground.

The service came to a halt and people huddled around Muddy, fanned her, and a nurse from Thomasville took her pulse and told the huddle that she was alive, probably just passed out from the heat. Muddy came around, got up, and made it back to the car with Lily and Todd supporting her, and Lily drove her home. Lily wanted to take her to the hospital, but Muddy refused: "I just need to rest."

"You sure, Mama? I would feel better if I took you for a quick check in the emergency room."

"Never been anything quick about an emergency room. I'm fine."

"Well, if you think so. I thought the service was nice," Lily said.

"Long time coming, but better than nothing at all."

Muddy heard later that night by phone from Lily that they had unveiled the marker and it was beautifully done in bronze and showed a picture of Cassie, her birth and death dates, and brief story. As Muddy rested in the lift chair, she imagined Cassie standing next to the marker, all these years later, touching, rubbing the raised bronze letters and smiling.

Chapter 2

In memory of Hispanic migrant farm workers who were murdered in 2005: Mateo Pais Gomez, Florindo Mauricio Pais, Jose Luiz Paez, Guadalupe Sanchez Cabello, Felipe Mauricio Esparza, and Armando Martinez Perez

Muddy sat up in her bed, the metal box springs creaking, and yawned. She felt pretty good and had slept well. Her heartbeats didn't feel as abnormal as they had yesterday, and her stomach growled. She craved a cup of coffee and thought bacon, eggs, and toast with Mayhaw jelly would be good for breakfast. After breakfast, Muddy carried a cup of coffee to her side table next to her lift chair and eased in to read the paper and watch the morning news.

She read the Cassie Harris marker dedication story in the paper and clipped it to put in the shoebox she kept in the cedar chest. When Muddy turned on the TV, the regional news channel out of Tallahassee, Florida was showing a breaking story out of Tifton, Georgia about a mass murder. At first, Muddy gulped. Her son Timothy lived there. He was the most financially successful of the bunch, she would often say because he had become a lawyer, though she often wondered about lawyers. She didn't like the way they could spin anything, good or bad. Timothy had been like that as a child, too, always putting a spin on what he'd done wrong: "Mama, the reason I knocked Lily down is because she looked like she was about to run into the street in front of a car," he'd once said. "There wasn't a car coming," Lily'd responded. "There might have been," Timothy'd said. She figured he'd turn out to be a car salesman and ultimately decided there wasn't much of a difference between lawyers and car salesmen, except a degree. Of course, Muddy loved him and would love him no matter what he did. Her late husband Claude hadn't gone to college at all, but Muddy had gone to the local agricultural college in Tifton where she'd taken several courses in Home Economics. She'd maintained friendships with those from her class back in the 1950s, but didn't get to see many of them through the years unless someone died, and she'd been to her fair share of funerals. One of her classmates still lived in Tifton, she remembered, and she hoped it wasn't her who'd been murdered. Surely, Timothy would've called her if Rebecca had been killed. They both go to church together at First Baptist, and Timothy always kept her up on any news from Rebecca.

Murder wasn't really all that shocking to her. It seemed to happen weekly, especially in some of the bigger towns and cities, and it seemed to be associated with people who were involved in something they shouldn't have been involved in: liquor, drugs, sex, or gambling. She thought the exceptions seemed to be women from abusive relationships, but mass murder was rare. She couldn't even recall when there had been one in South Georgia, except the Alday family in the 1970s. She remembered the Guyana tragedy and the Heaven's Gate incident from TV, but these were different because they were far off and involved suicide and not direct murder. Muddy felt like it didn't matter to God if one directly took someone's life or convinced him to take his own life. She felt killing was killing and someone would pay for that in the end.

When WCTV in Tallahassee went to commercial, Muddy switched channels on her remote to WALB out of Albany and continued to switch back and forth until she had a decent summary of the mass murder: Four black individuals, two female and two male, entered a migrant worker camp around one o'clock in the morning where they beat six Hispanic males with aluminum baseball bats and claw hammers and shot them to death. Several other Hispanic family members sustained multiple and critical injuries, including one of the victim's sister who was brutally raped and beaten. There was a gruesome shot of one of the men lying on the floor in a pool of blood with a claw hammer stuck in his head. The news anchor noted authorities suspected the murders were racially motivated and the home invasions were because of the large amounts of cash migrant workers keep at their homes since the workers were illegal and couldn't open bank accounts.

One Mexican woman was interviewed. She was beautiful with black hair, a cotton dress that looked faded and worn, and she was holding a baby with only a diaper. She tried to wipe tears and mumbled, "Los asesinos entraros sin resistencia porque las puertas no tenian candados, ni siquiera chapas, los golpearon y pataron para robarles su dinero. ellos vinieron aqui a trabajar, a ganar dinero y poder mantener a sus pobres familas en Mexico." The caption at the bottom read that the killers had gotten in because there was no knob or lock and that the poor victims had come here to work to send their earnings back to support their poor families in Mexico.

Muddy wondered how owners of these large farms could allow such living conditions for these families and still go to church on Sunday, if they even did. She understood the concept of capitalism, but in this instance, it certainly didn't seem fair. By the look of the camp, which certainly wouldn't be visible to anyone driving main roads, there were windows missing from the trailer, a box fan was propping one window up with duct tape on either side of the fan to cover the remaining space and to keep mosquitoes out. According to the reporter, there were ten to twelve migrant workers to a three bedroom single wide trailer, most of them sleeping on either single mattresses strewn about or in sleeping bags. One camera shot showed blood spatter in what ought to be a bathroom, but there was no toilet. The Port-O-Potty outside was their only facilities. Another shot panned the camp and showed a concrete slab by a light pole with a make shift spigot fashioned to the pole for running water, and Muddy shook her head in disgust at the bathing facilities. She suspected she knew the "farmer" who owned this camp and used, and abused, this cheap labor. She also knew he was taking a huge subsidy from the government and living as high on the hog as anyone in South Georgia with a big new home, new cars, trucks, and farming equipment. He also made sure no development was going to encroach onto his business and so he stayed heavily involved in the local Chamber and the Economic Development Board, which Muddy mused was less development than anti-development and self-protection. It disgusted her how the good old boy system was still in place in many areas and was primarily why South Georgia hadn't progressed as it could have.

In an update on the services for the victims, the reporter noted they would have a memorial at the All Saints Catholic Church in Tifton, but their bodies would be hauled in the back of a pick-up truck to Mexico where they would be buried. The reporter noted that insufficient funds were available for funeral home workers to transport them and that necessary paperwork had to be filed to take bodies out of state and country. Switching, the reporter noted the Mayor of Tifton had been presented a Mexican flag by the town's only Catholic priest, and the mayor had vowed to fly the flag at half-staff over the courthouse for six days, one day for each victim. This decision, in turn, the reporter noted, had apparently caused a controversy with some local whites who had complained mostly by a radio call-in show that it was inappropriate to fly another country's flag. One local man commented on camera: "They wouldn't fly the American flag in Mexico if one of us whites was murdered there."

"Idiot," Muddy commented, wondering why in the world television reporters seemed to find the stupidest people to interview. What she knew was this was a tragedy, that it may be the first local one she had encountered in her adult life. Apparently, the criminals had come from Moultrie and were after cash for drugs. The criminals had learned from a migrant worker they shared time with at the local rehabilitation hospital that migrant workers didn't have bank accounts and kept all their cash at home. Muddy grabbed the funeral home fan from the table and fanned. She felt the kerplunk in her chest, took a deep breath, and then felt okay.

These murders were geographically just too close, and it bothered her that these poor traveling migrant workers and their families, many of whom didn't even speak English, had been treated this way. She wondered how safe she was in her little town of Morven if some of these crazed drug addicts came to invade her home in the night. She knew what money she had was in the bank. Muddy wondered if somehow the politicians weren't to blame given they had made it illegal for migrant workers to have bank accounts and even further, she wondered if they ever fully realized or understood the implications of any of the laws they passed and policies they set. She recalled reading where it was illegal in Georgia for a chicken to cross the road, where a state Senator couldn't get a speeding ticket while the state's assembly was in session, and where one couldn't spit from a car while driving, among others, and this seemed to confirm that at least in some cases, the state legislature had no idea what it was doing. She knew they could certainly raise taxes on people while padding their own salaries and benefits, taking the lead from their Washington counterparts.

When the last commercial faded, a silly commercial with people dancing, gyrating this way and that, first in a park, then a laundry-mat, and finally a grocery store to illustrate how well an arthritis medication worked, Muddy thought hers hadn't improved when she had taken the medication. She knew she didn't feel like dancing anywhere. Muddy noted that most medication was like the elixirs (alcohol with food coloring) she'd taken as a child---their ability to heal was mostly in the mind. The body had a natural way of repairing itself with most things, but it wasn't a perfect system. Sometimes, though, it was too late, and beatings from baseball bats and claw hammers and shots from a semi-automatic weapon were too much for any healing process.

Still, Muddy knew in her heart that those migrant workers were going to a better place, a place where they had a beautiful home with door knobs, probably gold ones. There would no more blistered skin from work in the fields, no more hunger pangs, and no more worries about money. She didn't care if they were Catholic or not. Unlike some Protestants, Muddy believed Catholics were as much Christian as were those in her religion, just a little more formal with their beads, incense, and confessions.

The ringing of the phone startled her because she was so involved in her thoughts and the news report. "Hello?"

"Hey, Mama. You okay?" Timothy asked.

"Sure am. I'm just torn up about all these murders in Tifton."

"Yes mam, it's a pretty bad situation and we've apparently made national headlines."

"I hadn't even thought to watch national news this morning, but I'll switch over there and see what they're saying."

"Mostly, mama, I just wanted you not to worry."

"I 'preciate that."

"The GBI and the sheriff's department have the suspects in custody."

"It's a shame. Just a shame. I don't know when I've heard something so bad. You ain't gonna be their lawyer, are you?"

"No mam, but I may be called on to assist the D.A.'s office on contract given our firm's Spanish speaking abilities."

"Well, good. How's Nancy?"

"Fine. She stays busy with church and volunteering in the community. Ever since Hunter went off to college, she's been kind of depressed."

"She'll be alright. They call that empty nest syndrome. Saw it on Oprah last week."

"Well, she's worried about him doing well in college."

"He'll be fine. He's a smart boy and you did a good job raising him. He's probably more like you than his no count daddy was." Nancy's first husband had been killed in a drunk driving accident. Fortunately, he didn't kill anyone other than himself. He'd hit a tree head on doing about 80 miles per hour and no air bag was going to save him from that. She was working for Timothy at the time as a paralegal and he had helped her through the tragedy, and they became close. Timothy's first wife had left him after only a year of marriage, and Muddy was thankful they didn't have children. She was convinced the woman had married him thinking he had money, but young lawyers often don't, and she took flight when she realized he couldn't keep her in designer clothes from Atlanta.

"Yes mam, I know what you mean."

"You think these murderers will get off?"

"No, I think the evidence is probably stacked against them. It's just not clear who did what. Apparently, one of the women was the driver and didn't even get out of the car. They all agreed on that separately when they were questioned, and I think their stories indicate the other female assisted with the crimes, but didn't actually kill anyone. The two males, though, will certainly get life, if not the death penalty."

"I know I shouldn't say this, but I think they should have to suffer the way they made those poor migrant workers suffer."

"It's tough, no matter which way you look at it."

"Those pictures they showed this morning were awful."

"They shouldn't show that to increase ratings."

"And what about the farmer? Ought to put him on trial for making them live that way."

"That won't happen."

"Well, thanks for calling me."

"I hope we'll see you this weekend."

"Alright, then, bye-bye," Muddy said and turned off the phone.

When she hung up, she knew she wouldn't see them over the weekend. Rarely did they make the thirty minute drive to see her because they were too busy, and she didn't feel comfortable driving to see them either. Muddy knew she had turned a corner. She had less muscle mass, and while she wasn't fat, she had some flab. She also couldn't see as well. Part of that was not paying attention, becoming absorbed in her own thoughts to the extent that she would veer over the center line or off on the grass. One day, she had nearly flipped her Park Avenue and had to pull off just to catch her breath.

Muddy, in what she assumed might be her final days, had begun to think of humanity in general, and she had reached some general conclusions that at first, she mused, seemed rather depressing, but on reflection, were just her pragmatic thoughts and she would probably keep them to herself, unless she could pass them on to one of her two grandchildren, if they would come visit. First, she realized she had come in the world alone and would go out of the world alone. Next she had realized that most people aren't remembered once they were gone, contrary to the importance they tend to ascribe to themselves while alive. Her justification in thinking that was how many of her own family had gone on before her and how now, all these years later, she could barely remember them, and after her, there wouldn't be anyone to remember them at all. Her children had never known that generation of family. None of them had done great things in life like an Abraham Lincoln or a George Washington. They were just simple people, working and trying to survive until they couldn't. So, it had come to Muddy that what was truly important in a life was the relationships one has with others as well as what relationship one has with herself, and that the Golden Rule seemed to be the most applicable to all religions, philosophies, and positions, whether a believer in God or not. Muddy believed we should treat ourselves as we would have others treat us and we should extend that to all people. If only those criminals had believed this, we would have had no murders. The flaw, she felt, in humanity was that most people couldn't move beyond themselves. They didn't see we were all connected, like when she looked at a picture of Earth from space. There were no countries or states or counties or cities and even when one zoomed in further, she could see tons of people, just like we view ants marching to their hills. While most are working together to make the world what it is, some don't and do things against others. That's when the violations occur and that is the fall of humanity, the free will.

Chapter 3

In memory of the hundreds of victims at the Florida School for Boys at Marianna

Muddy didn't feel like watching TV at all, and she'd been thinking about dividing the photographs she kept in shoe boxes in the cedar chest of her bedroom. When she finally passed, Muddy didn't want her children to have to spend a lot of time dividing up or going through her things. She had a sense of what pieces of furniture they wanted and had once asked them to which they had replied, "Oh, Mama, that's silly talk. You've got a long way to go." Yet, Anthony, Timothy, and Lily had told her what they each wanted, adding, "Well, if that's alright with everybody," as if there were a line of heirs. Muddy had gotten them to tape a piece of paper underneath most of the furniture with their names on it. It was too much on her knees to squat and do it herself.

When she got to the bedroom, she pulled a straight back chair from the pencil-legged desk to the front of the cedar chest and sat. She opened the lid until it stayed propped against the footboard of her double bed, and she pulled shoeboxes and put them on the patchwork quilt her grandmother had made when she was a child (Lily would get this when Muddy passed; though it wasn't labeled, everyone understood). Once the boxes were unloaded, Muddy pulled the chair to the side of the bed, walked over to the desk, and turned on the radio to W.A.F.T., the local gospel station and sat in the straight back chair grabbing the first shoe box. "Shall We Gather at the River" was playing, and as Muddy went through the photos, she hummed along with the song. She found pictures of her grandparents, good and hard-working farmers from over in the edge of Lanier County and buried at Wayfare Primitive Baptist Church right next to the river, and she recalled going to church with them in their buggy once for dinner on the grounds. One reason she recalled this so well was because she'd been fascinated by their church's practice of baptism by immersion in the river once a quarter. She had only experienced the practice of Baptism, by what some referred to as "sprinkling" as an infant in the Methodist church, but figured it didn't matter if you got a little or a lot as long as you were saved.

Muddy noted a picture of Claude and her, just married, at the Methodist church in Thomasville. They had been a handsome couple, full of energy and with all sorts of opportunities before them. Time had passed quickly for them with Claude working at the dairy outside Thomasville before getting a job at the coat factory, now closed, and the old red brick building remodeled to rent out for special events. Muddy looked at her hair, jet black and sprayed stiff as a board, her lean and milky white skin and the small diamond Claude had bought for her on lay-away at the jewelry store in Thomasville. She still wore the diamond, but her milky white skin had long since been changed into spots and wrinkles that no amount of lotions and creams could change back, despite their ads on TV. She noted in the photo the first car she and Claude had driven, a Nash Metropolitan convertible, teal and white. Muddy had loved that car and felt so special learning to drive it. She remembered how Anthony and Timothy would hang the arms over the side, moving their hands up and down as if surfers on the wind. They finally traded it for a Chevrolet Impala when Lily was born. The Nash was just too cramped for the growing family.

She found an Easter photo with Timothy and Anthony by the Azaleas in the front yard. Anthony, the first born, had his shirt buttons all fastened while Timothy had his top button undone. It struck her that they were so different. She was so afraid when pregnant with Anthony and was cautious about every move she made, but by the time she was pregnant with Timothy, she was much more care free. Muddy hadn't rushed to clean up spills or pick up knocked over knick-knacks as much with Timothy as she had been with Anthony. She felt that reflected in their personalities as babies with Anthony having colic and being fussy while Timothy was more playful and happy. Anthony hadn't married and lived alone in Thomasville. He was overly neat, as Muddy mentioned to friends, a result of a little nervous energy he always had. He managed the Piggly Wiggly and worked long hours. He had started there as a bag boy when he was in high school, had learned how to stock shelves, rotating the older items toward the front, and clean (of course, Muddy had taught him that). At some point after high school, he had been promoted to a supervisor and later after the manager retired, the manager. The store was always clean, and while newer stores with fancy delis, high-end items, and even organic sections had come to be popular in Thomasville and other towns, the Piggly Wiggly had become a mainstay, an icon of things past that were well maintained. They continued to have a lot of customers, mostly blue collar workers and elderly people, and continued to turn a profit.

Muddy put the pictures in different stacks and then she figured she'd begin to refill the shoeboxes and write each of her three children's names on them. As she moved one stack to a box for Anthony, she noted a tear drop. "Nonsense," she muttered. She told herself to stop feeling sorry for herself and getting emotional. She knew she'd had a good life and she might even be around a few years longer. Muddy didn't feel talking about how one felt was all that great and noted in her day, a simple look or gesture communicated more than words. Raised eyebrows, pursed lips, or a pointed finger from her parents sent messages to Muddy and her siblings that needed no words. She felt people talked too much now and reckoned TV was to blame. That and the 1960s when women quit wearing bras, free-love was in, and teens let themselves go, looking sloppy and unkempt. Lily'd been a teenager then, and while she bought and listened to some of the folk music on albums or eight-track, Muddy wasn't going to have her acting like one of them hippies. Actually, Muddy had liked some of the music. She liked Simon and Garfunkel; Peter, Paul, and Mary; Joan Baez; and the Mama's and the Papa's. Muddy thought Mama Cass had one of the best voices ever, and when Joan Baez sang "Diamonds in the Rust," she got goose bumps on her arms. That was it, though. She didn't like the rest of them, especially that scruffy smart aleck Bob Dylan. She couldn't believe someone had let him in a recording studio let alone cut multiple records, given his nasal voice.

Muddy found a photo of her as a child on a pony, and she found one of Claude on a pony as well. She noted that people didn't travel around the rural countryside any longer taking pictures of children on ponies and it must be because that's no longer in vogue. Back then, Roy Rogers, Dale Evans, John Wayne were world famous, along with other cowboys and cowgirls, and this was a popular thing to have done. In one of the shoeboxes, Muddy noted there were several letters. She didn't recall having saved letters. She knew the biggest shoebox was her newspaper clippings. One of the letters was to Muddy and Claude from Anthony at 4-H Camp in Rock Eagle. She had recognized his perfect hand-writing immediately. As she read it, she smiled. It was Anthony's first trip away from home, and he was swimming and he was part of the Cherokee tribe at the camp. He told Muddy the food wasn't as good as hers and she chuckled. Anthony had been the pleaser of the three. Timothy, on the other hand, had been the manipulator of the three. Muddy often felt she couldn't resist his sweet smile and innocent look when it came to punishment. She mostly let Claude handle that. Lily, of course, had been a daddy's girl and was a tomboy. Any dress Muddy made or bought wasn't quite what Lily had in mind, opting for shorts or jeans and tennis shoes most of her life. It wasn't until she became an adult that she wore more dresses. Of course, she wore them to church as a child. All girls did then, but it was all Muddy could do to keep them clean.

There were a few envelopes that consisted of birthday cards, sympathy cards when Muddy's mother had passed, other letters from friends, but one letter stood out in a child's writing with the return address of Florida Boys School in Marianna, Florida. Muddy had never been there, didn't recall a relative being sent there, or anyone from church. She opened it, and it was a letter to her children from a Holloway boy who had once lived down the road and was a classmate of Anthony's, though Muddy recalled he had a crush on Lily and played more outside with Timothy. His daddy had died in a drunken brawl in Tallahassee, and he was being raised by his mother, but she remarried a man who beat the boy, and he was sent away. Muddy thought he'd gone to live with relatives, not sent to a boys' school, but reflected he may have gone to relatives who then sent him. She just didn't recall and she didn't actually recall the letter either, but there was something about his tone that gave her chills:

Dear Tim, Lily, and Anthony,

I hope ya'll doin' good. I'm in Florida at the boys school. I sure wish ya'll could come git me so I could live there agin. I know ya'll eat good and has got a good mama and daddy, like angels. There ain't an angel here less it's them that died and buried out back with no graves. They took it long as they could, I reckon. I slipped and said sumthin' I shouldn'ta said and I got beat pretty bad. Old fat nurse with a black cat patched me up some, but some of my sores ain't healed yet. I just pray I don't git sent back to the white house no more. That's where they do it, the beatin and all. Shame it's called the white house. I'm awful weary and need rest. It's hard to sleep at night knowing somebody's gittin' beat or worse. I didn't get worse, but some boys do. They scared to tell anybody cause others gone missin. My letter might never git to ya'll either, but I'm gonna sneak out in the night and throw it in the blue metal bin. I hope it gits out. If they catch me tryin to mail it, I might git another beatin. When I first got here after my mama's husband beat me, I thought it was gonna be great. They got a pool and a basketball kort. Cain't nobody hardly play or do nothin. You got to be quite and read or act like it. Anything other than that, you git beat. Mama came once, but she didn't see nothing. I tried to tell her, but they don't let you visit long. I ain't seen Mama but that one time. I'm afeared that man done beat her too. If ya'll could come for me, I promise I'd earn my keep and even get a job and quit skool. I still look the same, but they knocked some teeth out my mouth, so I ain't got that Holloway smile no more. I'm sure ya'll been busy with skool and church. I sure do miss Morven and I never thought I'd say that. Even church. I hope to hear from ya'll soon. I'm prayin.

Yur friend,
Hank Holloway

Muddy felt cold and clammy. She felt another kerplunk. She wondered if the children had read the letter. She wondered if Claude read it. She didn't recall Claude ever saying anything about it. Surely, Hank was putting on and making things worse than they were. She was thinking the boy must have been about eight years old when this occurred. Muddy placed the letter on the quilt and then picked it up and read it again. The letter had been opened, so she figured that one of the children must have read it and thought it was a joke. Or, maybe they had actually asked her about it and she was busy in the kitchen or cleaning something and shooed them away, like a pesky gnat. Sometimes, she just replied, "Yes, yes," or "Marvelous," and they'd be off and into something else. One time, they pushed her in a corner. She'd been busy cooking, Claude was still at work, and they came running in the kitchen, tracking mud and grass on her freshly mopped floor, and got her so flustered that when they asked for chocolate pudding for desert, she said, "Yes, yes; now, get out of my kitchen. Ya'll are making a mess." When Claude came in, they told him she was making chocolate pudding, which he thought odd given Muddy never made pudding from scratch, only pies and cakes. Muddy had said she never said anything like that, and the children out-voted her. Claude had to drive down to the Suwannee Swifty to pick up ice cream to calm everyone. The ideas of children come and go, and she could easily have ignored a question about Hank coming to live with them. She certainly hoped she didn't, but she made up her mind to call the boys and find out.

Timothy's office manager answered. "Why, yes, Mrs. Rewis, he's here."

"Hey, Mama. You alright?"

"I'm okay, but I'm worried about this boy, Hank Holloway."

"Hank Holloway?"

"You remember him?"

"Yeah, I do. He lived down the road from us when we were in elementary school. Did he die or something? You usually don't call me at work unless someone has died."

"I don't like bothering you at work unless it's important." Muddy continued. "I don't know if he's dead or not. I found a letter he wrote."

"Recently?"

"No, when he was a boy. Remember, he went away, and we thought he'd been sent to stay with relatives after his mother remarried. He might have, but he ended up at this school for boys in Marianna, Florida, and Timothy, they beat and abused him. He wrote to us asking if we'd come get him and let him live with us. He alluded to murders. Do you remember this letter?"

"Mama, I really don't remember anything like that. Maybe he did write us a letter. Was it to just me or to all of us?"

"It was addressed to all three of you."

"You think Anthony opened it and read it?"

"He would have said something. Actually, he would have said something several times."

Timothy chuckled. "That's right. I'll tell you what, Mama. I'll do some internet searches and see if I can turn up Hank. I'll even contact him if I can find him."

"Well, that would make me feel a little better. I know it's been forty or so years, but this bothers me that me and your daddy missed this. I don't know how it ended up in the shoe box."

"Why was it in a shoebox?"

"Oh, I had some other letters and photos in one box. I've been going through all the pictures to divide them up for ya'll, so you don't have to worry about that when I pass."

"Mama, that's silly talk. You've got years."

Muddy dismissed his remarks. "You got time to check on that boy now?"

"Well, I was in the middle of something, but I could use a break. Let me see what I can find out and I'll call you back in about thirty minutes."

"Alright, I'll be here."

Muddy knew he wouldn't call back in thirty minutes. Timothy had never been on time in his life. She believed it was a miracle he was successful at all, but a smile and apology seemed to work for him and take him places. She would expect his call in an hour or so.

They hung up, and Muddy busied herself about the bedroom labeling shoeboxes and continuing to go through pictures. She came across one of the family at Disney World. It was one of the few vacations they all enjoyed. Most of the time, they went to the beach, got sunburned, ate a lot of sandwiches, got sand on everything, and someone usually got stung by a jellyfish or by a yellow jacket. She thanked God none of them ever drowned at Fernandina Beach in the undertow. They'd known people who drowned. In fact, the minister of the Baptist church had been drowned by the undertow. He was attempting to save someone who was drowning and he did, but in the process, he drowned himself. It was a tragedy for the Baptists of Morven, and some had moved to the Methodist church because they didn't feel they could go back there. Muddy felt that was a silly reason to switch religions, but believed to each his own.

What her family loved most about Disney World was the monorail. It was like riding a bullet through the sky, and it seemed so sleek and modern. They'd never seen anything like it. They couldn't afford to stay in the modern hotel the monorail glided through on its way to the magic kingdom with its castle entrance. The magic was definitely there. From the animals and characters from Disney movies to the perfectly manicured gardens to the fancy rides, Disney had taken the notion of rural fair or carnival to a new level and all the while making folks feel safe and care-free. Muddy, who didn't like rides, had even ridden the race cars and the shuttle to the future. She loved the boats in "It's a Small World," but they could never make up their mind which was the favorite ride of all: "Jungle Cruise" or the "Paddlewheel Riverboat." Both were wonderful adventures and seemed as if they had gone down the mighty Mississippi and the Amazon.

When Timothy finally called, some three hours later, Muddy had already eaten a banana sandwich and drank tea for lunch. She had thawed a pack of lady finger peas and put them on low to cook in chicken broth to have with her baked barbeque chicken for supper. She was getting a little tired and wanted to take a short nap.

"Hello?" Muddy answered the phone.

"Hey, Mama. Sorry it took me so long. Something came up I had to deal with."

"That's alright," she said. She had long since accepted his behavior, though it still annoyed her.

"I found several Hank Holloways online, but none of them seem to fit our Hank."

Muddy had no idea what he was talking about. "What do you mean you found several and they weren't him?"

"Mama, I am running a search using the computer. It identifies several people with that name, but none of them, as I find them, are about his age or are from Georgia. Some are even a difference race."

"Well, I believe you. I just didn't understand. Does that mean he died?"

"Maybe, or maybe not. What I can do through my legal connections is make a couple of calls to friends in Florida who may know where I can see the burial list for that area. If it's a state facility, then they have to maintain a cemetery listing. If that is available, then we might be able to determine if he's in there or not."

"In his letter, he indicates some of the boys have been killed by the staff and buried and not recorded."

"Oh, Mama, Hank was always exaggerating and making things up. The letter is probably made up, too. He was probably just trying to get back to Morven, so he could spend time with Lily. I think he just befriended me to get to Lily."

"Well, check on it today and call me this evening. I'm gonna take a little nap. This whole letter has got me tied up in knots."

"Mama, just rest. You don't need to worry about that at all. It's probably nothing."

Muddy was fairly tired and once she hung up the phone, she laid down and covered up with her quilt. The coolness of the antique backing of the quilt always gave her an immediate comfortable feeling that may have been more psychological than real, and she fell asleep quickly. She awoke to the sound of the doorbell and struggled to gain her composure, grab her cane and get there. She opened the wood door and said "Hey" to Anthony and unlatched the screen door.

"Mama, I was getting worried."

"I was taking a nap. How come you ain't at work?"

"Well, I switched my days around some and today was my day off. I cleaned and worked in the yard this morning. Had lunch at the Plaza during Rotary and then ran some errands. Thought I would ride over here and see if I could take you out for supper."

"You should've called me. I've already thawed chicken and have peas on the stove."

"That'll keep till tomorrow. Why don't you ride over to Ray's Mill Pond and let's eat fish?"

"That does sound good. I think I'll take you up on it. I'm glad you came. I want to show you this letter and see if you remember anything about that boy ya'll were friends with named Hank Holloway."

Muddy made her way to the bedroom, Anthony trailing behind, and she grabbed the letter and directed Anthony to read it.

"Goodness, this sounds awful," he said. "This is from the sixties and it was in a shoebox?"

"Yes," she said. "I would have put it there, but I don't recall reading this, nor do I recall you all saying anything about it."

"This sounds pretty bad, Mama. I vaguely remember this boy."

"Yeah, I think he was your age, but he mainly played with Timothy, and I think he might have had a crush on Lily. I've got your brother checking to see what he can find out. See if he's still alive or not. You don't recall anything at all?"

"No, I really don't. Maybe we read it and thought it was a joke, so he could get back here to see Lily. We heard them in the barn and caught them kissing."

"Kissing? Lord, ya'll didn't tattle on her? Her daddy would have whipped her behind for such, but I hate we didn't pay attention to the letter. That me and your daddy didn't even talk about it."

After Muddy got ready, Anthony pulled the car into the yard near the porch, so Muddy didn't have so far to walk. They rode over to Berrien County to Ray's Mill Pond, which had been a conglomeration of shacks attached together on the edge of the cypress pond. Now, it's much more modern and even has air conditioning. Muddy had tried their fried gator tail, but she preferred fried catfish sprinkled with lemon juice. Anthony, the weight watcher of her bunch, would have broiled fish—mullet or perch. Muddy probably shouldn't be eating fried foods, but she wasn't much worried about it anymore. On the ride home, Anthony suggested they stop in Hahira at the Dairy Queen and get an ice cream.

"I don't need that, and you didn't have to buy my supper. I should've bought yours. You're the one with bills."

"Not any more. I paid off my house last week, finally. It feels good. That's why I'm celebrating."

"Congratulations! Your daddy would be proud, too."

"Thanks, Mama. I think I'm gonna stop anyway and get me a vanilla cone. You want one?"

"Alright. Get me a chocolate. I shouldn't, really, because dairy upsets my stomach, but one scoop won't hurt."

They sat in the car, the curb attendant bringing it out. Other than the employees, this DQ hadn't changed much over time. Muddy had good memories of Hahira and clearly remembered coming with her daddy to sell tobacco at one of the many warehouses by the railroad track. She looked forward to the day she got to see her daddy again.

When Anthony and Muddy got back to Morven, they pulled in and she told her son to come inside in case Timothy had called and left a message.

"Mama, the light is blinking on your answering machine."

"Push the play button and see who it is." Timothy's voice was on the machine asking his mother to call, so she grabbed the phone and called him at home. She knew he wouldn't still be in his office, which was something she thought was good. He didn't always work long hours unless it was absolutely necessary.

"Hey, Mama," Timothy said, once she got him to the phone.

"Hey. Anthony is here with me. We rode over to Ray's Mill Pond and ate fish."

"I figured you had a date," he responded.

"Don't be smart. What did you find out about that boy?"

"Well, it seems there might have been some truth to his letter. Apparently, the Florida School for Boys has a rather notorious history and has been investigated several times through the years by various agencies. The Civil Rights division of the Justice department investigated allegations of abuses, murders, rapes, and other crimes, and much of this was confirmed by other investigations as well. Many who worked there and had run the school maintained the allegations are not true. Surprise inspections found boys hogtied and several in leg irons. Some maintained they were placed in handcuffs and hung from ceilings for hours at a time. If that ain't bad enough, the number of recorded graves is around thirty, but recent investigations using radar reflects that there might be well over fifty graves. A few years back, some of the survivors tried to sue, but there wasn't enough evidence and the statute of limitations had expired. Of course, there's no statute of limitations for murder, so if they exhume bodies and determine murder, they will pay for those crimes, if they are still living, of course.

"What about Hank Holloway?" Muddy asked.

"No record of him in the cemetery, Mama. They have a record of him checking into the facility, but no discharge record. So, I'd say it's likely he might be one of the undocumented graves, unless there's just an error from staff about him having left. I guess it'll always be a mystery, Mama."

Muddy shook her head, looking at Anthony. "I reckon one day we'll know the truth. Then it won't matter."

Timothy and Muddy said goodbye, and Muddy said she didn't feel good. She hoped Hank Holloway wasn't in an unmarked grave, having suffered and died for someone else's sins of the mind, and she felt guilty. She felt like that ice cream might come rushing up, but she knew that wouldn't alleviate the guilt she felt for not having read that letter and acted. She told Anthony she'd like for him to take her to the Marianna home, so she could see the place in person, and she knew in her mind that when Anthony took her that she would shout out to Hank Holloway that she had finally come, that she was sorry she was so late, that he could've come and lived with them, and that she would have treated him as if he were her own child.

That night, Muddy dreamed of the children rushing into the kitchen when she was trying to cook and handing her the mail. She glanced at the paper and a letter, opened it, but as she did, the kettle whistled a little and then louder, and she set it aside next to a clean stack of dish rags, which she later crammed into a drawer when she was wiping counter crumbs. She went on cooking and setting the table as Claude came in and gave her a kiss on the cheek. He even gave her a little pat on her behind. "Stop that and go wash up," she said.

"Get anything in the mail, Muddy?"

"Just the paper. You can read it after supper."

Muddy turned, the bed creaked and she briefly opened her eyes, and then closed them feeling the cotton backing on the quilt her grandmother had made.

Chapter 4

In memory of Helen Griffin Hanks
who disappeared in Southern Georgia in 1972 and whose
remains were unearthed from a field in 1980

Muddy didn't often go to the Suwannee Swifty on the corner about a block from her house, though she passed it constantly on her way to church or anywhere heading east on highway 122, but she was out of milk and didn't want to make a trip to Thomasville for a small carton. She used the milk in her Corn Flakes, she used it to cook biscuits or pies, and she warmed it at night to drink before bed, but not a lot because it bothered her. She believed it helped her sleep, and she also believed that's why her bones had held up all these years and her friends' bones hadn't. She couldn't count the number of friends who'd broken their hips or were humped over from osteoporosis.

She didn't like driving to the store either, preferring to walk, but it was dusk and she was afraid of crime. Morven didn't have major crime exactly, but they had what others called no count young people who were not educated, not working, and had nothing else to do but put their energy to finding ways to get into trouble, getting what they wanted. She imagined them to be like Robin Hood's band of merry men, staying up half the night and feeding off of each other's wildness. These teens were what she'd often associated with the "least of these" she'd heard in sermons at First Methodist, but no one seemed to ever help them on a local level, preferring instead to send their funds to missionary work in countries that hate America, which was no different than elected officials in Washington. To Muddy, all this giving to others in countries wasn't going to make much of a difference overseas, exhibited by the flag burning and protests she saw on TV almost weekly. She felt sending resources overseas was taking away from what we could do to better our own country and was going to ultimately destroy America, unintentionally, of course. In fact, she had gone so far as to tell the preacher anything she gave to the church better not be used for mission work, and she speculated he thought she had a mean streak for having said that. It wasn't often she got riled up about something, but sometimes she got to dwelling on something so much that she just seemed to get angry. It's like it continued to well-up inside her and spill over, like a clogged toilet. The result could make a mess. The preacher avoided her for a couple of weeks; she noticed the way he flashed his eyes her way and then turned to engage someone as she neared. She knew the cornerstone of the Methodist church was in missions, and she didn't mind missionaries telling people about Jesus, but she didn't like sending all this aid year after year that had become dependency.

Muddy understood that the crime in Morven were petty ones like theft. She knew things had gone missing from the barn, and she had finally asked Anthony to put a lock on the barn door, but she still felt people could get in there. Once she'd called the police when she saw a boy going in there, and they found him and brought him out, gave him a warning, and sent him on his way. She knew how people held grudges and remembered things, and she feared the boy would come back and do something else, maybe worse, but he never did. She didn't recall behavior like that when she was young and living on the farm with her family, but her fear was ever present now that she was alone. She believed that people became more afraid and crime rates rose because of a number of things, but she thought number one would be TV, going twenty-four hours a day, and blasting one crime after another whether it was local or in another country on the other side of the planet. The only two programs she found informative were Charles Kuralt on CBS Sunday Morning, where he often did features on what Muddy considered pleasant and interesting stories, and then 60 Minutes, a news show that did all sorts of interesting stories, in addition to Andy Rooney, who was funny to her. She thought he was cranky and a little financially tight, but she admired those qualities in a person and felt like more people ought to be that way.

When Muddy pulled the Buick into the parking space by the bagged ice machine, she nearly ran up on the curb because her foot slipped off the brake. The car jolted forward and then bounced back off the concrete lip of the store's porch, and Muddy was embarrassed. "You're alright," she heard Claude whisper. She put the car in park and switched off the ignition, reaching her left hand to her neck, which had popped. As she collected herself to get out of the car and moved her hand to the door handle, she noted a black woman with dread locks standing at her door and she felt that kerplunk in her chest briefly. She was startled. She opened the door, and the woman said, "You alright, Ms. Rewis?"

"Yes, I am. Thank you for asking."

"I thought you was gonna drive right through the glass and into the store. I didn't know if something had happened to you or not."

"My foot slipped off the brake."

"Oh. Well, I'm glad you's alright."

"Me, too."

"We'll be seein' you."

"Alright then," Muddy said. She recognized the woman as Crazy Jenny. Well, her name wasn't really Crazy Jenny, but that's what everyone called her. She'd always been a little off, having been born that way, but she was sweet and a hard worker from what everyone said. Crazy Jenny had gone to school with Lily, actually, and had graduated with a special diploma. Back then, everyone graduated whether students had gained any knowledge or not. They were simply promoted and pushed on toward some final education destination, and the light at the end of that tunnel was often a train, being hit by the reality that their diplomas meant nothing in Morven or anywhere else in the world if they couldn't read and write, and this was highlighted even more as the shirt factory over in Hahira and the coat factory over in Thomasville sent jobs South to Mexico. Crazy Jenny had even been to the Rewis home when she was young for a birthday party, and even then, Muddy had watched her and knew she wasn't all there. Rumor had it that her daddy had beaten her mama while she was pregnant with Jenny and maybe she had sustained some damage in the womb. It didn't matter now because Jenny was grown, her mama and daddy long dead, and she didn't even know she wasn't all there.

Muddy thought she'd really put the weight on, and her white clam digger pants were wedged in her butt crack, but Muddy thought it was interesting the way she moved. She seemed rather comfortable with her weight, her cheeks bouncing up and down and her long ear rings swaying in unison with her hands as she glided across the parking lot, through the vacant lot where a boarding house once stood, now a lot grown up with trash and busted glass, and on by the nursery full of trees and day lilies to the small housing project that had built in the 1960s for the "least of these." The project, which at the time seemed to have an elderly focus, had turned into multi-generational housing for the poor. Muddy imagined it to be like a wire trap used by hunters to catch opossums, raccoons, and armadillos; the project lured unsuspecting folks in and never released them, prisoners of a society doomed to repeat the cycle of poverty generation after generation.

While Muddy didn't like going into the Suwannee Swifty because she said it had a smell that was on her clothes when she came out, she did like the suction of the doors to the cooler, opening and closing quick and tight. She was suspect of the Indian who ran the store. His hair was always greasy, he smelled of curry, and he seemed to have an air of disgust and superiority which he exhibited toward his customers. She suspected he had a very low interest loan from the federal government to buy the store in Morven to begin with when local folks couldn't have access to such business loans, or if they did, they certainly didn't know how to get one. Muddy also thought he wore too much gold jewelry and what he wore was rather gaudy. She paid him in cash and he asked, "Lotto ticket?"

"No," Muddy said. "Just the milk." She wondered how many Georgia lottery tickets he sold on a daily basis, another program she didn't support. Of course, Muddy believed that people had the right to spend their money, or waste it, any way they chose, but the odds were against them. Yet, she'd heard conversations from others in public places that seemed to indicate the lottery created a false sense of hope among people. She also thought it was a cheap way out for the State of Georgia to shift funds typically used for Education out of one budget and replace it with lottery sales revenue, sending the traditional Education funds into another budget for special projects for legislators with the most political pull. As a result, Georgia had seen new buildings in many communities, multi-purpose space not used and named for prominent folks who had done nothing whatsoever in their communities.

Once back at home, Muddy poured a cup of milk into a pan to warm it and sip before going to sleep. She made sure the doors were locked before she went to the bedroom, put on her nightgown, pulled the covers back, and propped up on pillows to read and sip her milk. Muddy felt sad she was all alone in her last years and mused why so many elderly lose their hearing is because they don't need it anymore with children grown and gone. She wondered about heaven, if she would reunite with Claude, or if the new soul form would even be recognizable. She wondered if she would get to meet famous people she'd admired, like Franklin Roosevelt. She knew that like most politicians, he wasn't probably as good as the perception she and her parents had had of him, particularly given the rumors he'd stopped the train in Aiken, South Carolina at the Wilcox Inn to visit one of his main girlfriends on his way to the Little White House in Georgia. Some rumors had indicated Roosevelt didn't die at the Little White House and instead died at the Wilcox with his lover and was put on the train stiff as a board and hauled to the Little White House to avoid scandal. She knew God forgave sins like this and was thankful. She imagined Roosevelt's soul in heaven would not be crippled like his body had been on Earth, and she was comforted by the thought the aches and pains she felt would be gone, her friends would be healed from their osteoporosis, and those souls traumatized by their lives being taken unnaturally would be angels. With this, Muddy took one last sip of milk, laid her Guidepost on the side table, and turned off the lamp. She pulled the covers to her waist and rubbed the bottoms of her feet against the back of the quilt her grandmother had made and fell fast asleep.

The phone startled Muddy and she rubbed her eyes. The sun was already up and shining through the blinds in her bedroom. She sat up and grabbed the handset. "Hello." Her voice was hoarse from sleeping and snoring with her mouth open.

"Mama, you alright? How come it took you so long to answer?

"I'm fine. I'm just getting up."

"You sure you're alright? This ain't like you to sleep so late."

"What time is it, Lily?"

"Little past 8:00 a.m."

"That is late for me. I guess I must've needed the sleep."

"I guess you haven't seen the news then."

"No, what is it? They find that boy?"

"What boy?"

"The one who liked you when you were little. Hank Holloway."

"Mama, I don't know what you're talking about. You sure you're alright?"

"I'm fine. That boy that lived down the road that used to play with ya'll when ya'll were little was named Hank Holloway. I found a letter from him in a shoe box with photographs. He got sent away to the Florida School for the Boys. He wrote to us, asking for help, to come live with us. They beat them boys. Some died and got buried in unmarked graves on the property. There've been investigations for years. I talked to both your brothers about it. I thought one of them would've told you. I just forgot to call you about it."

"Oh, Mama, that's awful. Was he killed?"

"We don't know. There's no record of him checking out and no record of a grave, but he could be in one of them unmarked graves."

"Mama, you don't need to worry about that. You can't change the past."

"I know, I know, but it bothers me no one remembers the letter and ever did anything."

"If he was killed, Mama, he's better off in heaven, and they'll catch them and make them pay for what they did to him and other boys. Just like they're gonna get that murderer who killed Mae Jeter Pipkin. They found her remains, or what they assume to be her remains, late last night chopped up in a box and buried in a field. The box was a child's wood coffin box, the kind they ship caskets in to funeral homes. An old farmer turned it up when plowing, called the Sheriff, and it was on TV late last night and again this morning. They went straight to the funeral home to talk to the owner and his son, the main suspects, Melvin and Jeffrey West. "

"Mercy. I knew those rumors about her running off weren't true. What pain them Pipkin children have suffered all these years. How long has it been, Lily?"

"I think it's been twenty-something years, Mama."

"Thanks for letting me know. They were members of our church, so they'll be a lot to do this week. I'll check with some of my Sunday school members. Most likely, we'll prepare some food, and if they have a service, I'll try and go to that, too."

"I figured you might. I think it's just a shame. I don't guess they would ever forget their mama, or Mr. Pipkin, his wife, but I think finding out this way on the news has just got to disturb them forever. Of course, if she was just missing or had run off, I guess there was always some glimmer of hope she'd come home, that she was alive, but this news closes that door."

"It closes that door, but opens others, like who did it and why? And all these years, a murderer was on the loose."

"I think they suspect the younger West at the funeral home. There are rumors around Valdosta that he's crazy."

"Wouldn't surprise me, none," Muddy said. "Plenty of people over there are, but they've got some money. His mama was a Perry and they owned part of the hospital, and I think the older West's daddy owned a bank down town. He might just get off."

"I sure hope not."

"Me, too."

"Well, I'll let you go. I'll check on you later this week."

"Thank you for calling. Tell the boys hello."

"I will."

Muddy knew the gossip train had left the station last night and was probably still moving swiftly. She determined to call some of her Sunday School class members, and of course, as she made the calls, she learned everyone had either seen the news on TV or had been told by someone else in the class. Muddy, not prone to gossip, wasn't often in the loop, and that was fine with her. She preferred to avoid being tangled in spider webs.

A few days after Mae Jeter Pipkin's remains were returned from the Crime Lab in Atlanta, the family changed funeral homes to Thomasville, even though company policy at the West's funeral home was a free funeral for all employees. Muddy didn't blame the family one bit, and as it turned out, the Wests offered to pick up the tab from Thomasville, but Mr. Pipkin wouldn't hear of it and paid the bill himself.

Muddy prepared a casserole to take to the lunch after the funeral service at First Methodist, and she was there to help them serve, and as usual, the ladies did a great job. The Pipkin family told them how appreciative they were, and while there was obvious sadness during the service and after at the grave site, there was also a sense of closure. Muddy wasn't sure how one closed the door when a family member was murdered and brutally treated in such a way, but she vowed she would follow the investigation, and as the months passed, Muddy followed it closely by watching TV updates and reading *The Valdosta Daily Times*, to which she had a subscription. Additional sources came from the minister's wife, who went daily to Valdosta for the trial and reported back to her friend who was head of the Women's Methodist Union at their church, who, in turn, reported it to others who also reported it. Much of the news reported this way was also confirmed by one of the jurors who had a cousin who lived in Morven and went to the Methodist church and was married to one of the women in Muddy's Sunday School class. Of course, the juror wasn't supposed to talk, since there was a gag order, but Muddy and everyone else in South Georgia knew that such an order, even from a judge, whether he was elected or appointed, meant nothing. People were going to talk. They told it to others in a variety of forms: "Don't say I said it," or "If you can keep this quiet, I'll tell you something," or "I won't admit I told this, but."

And, as proved true over the next several months, the assault, sexual assault, and murder of Mae Jeter Pipkin turned out, in some ways, to be a fiasco. First, it was learned that the younger West, Jeffrey, who had been nicknamed Ice by friends in college, had apparently been caught in the act of having sex with corpses at the funeral home on more than one occasion. In fact, it was assumed that Mae Jeter Pipkin had somehow learned of this, informed Jeffrey West's father, and had threatened to turn him in for his disturbing behavior. The father pleaded the fifth when called to the stand and was of no use to the prosecution. Jeffrey West's ex-wife, however, turned out to be a gold mine. She testified that Jeffrey West had forced her to stand in front of the air conditioning before they had sex and pretended to be dead. He also hit her during these acts. She had become afraid of him and left, later filing for a no contested divorce. Another theory purported that Mr. West had made sexual advances toward Mae Jeter Pipkin even though she was married. Ambrose, a retired fellow who often assisted with funerals, greeting family and friends attending visitation, driving the hearse, and assisting with the coffin at the burial had testified he'd walked into the office one day while Jeffrey had Mae pinned up against a filing cabinet, his hands behind her on her buttocks while he rubbed against her. She held a lone file folder in her hand, attempted to push him away, and papers had dropped all over the floor. Ambrose testified that he'd stepped back from the entrance, cleared his throat a couple of times, heard the shuffling, and peaked in asking if he was interrupting anything to which West replied, "Of course, not." He walked to his office, shutting the door, while Mae was picking up paper off the floor.

"I'm sorry, Mr. Ambrose," she'd said. "It's been a trying day."

"Yes, mam," he'd said.

Ambrose told the court that it was clear to him that Mr. West's advances to Mae were unwanted and out of line. Of course, the defense attorney, one of the most expensive in the Southeast, had given Mr. Ambrose a difficult time, making him feel as if he were interpreting behavior and asserted it was Mae who welcomed these advances. Mr. Pipkin was called to the stand and basically said his wife had complained about some of the younger West's behavior—mainly that he often looked at her chest instead of making eye contact with her, that he'd also used inappropriate language in front of her. He told the court he was concerned about the situation and had encouraged her to talk with older Mr. West. The defense attorney, the paper had reported, did not question Mr. Pipkin because it wouldn't sit well with a jury and would seem disrespectful.

When Muddy heard this, she made her disgusting "Hmmph" sound, noting that the blame is often heaped upon the victims when they aren't here to defend themselves or give their version of reality. Mainly, she believed what the daughter had said during the eulogy: that her mother was an angel, that this world was not her home. The husband, children, and other family members never believed for a minute Mae Jeter Pipkin had run off with someone or had left them. They always believed there had been foul play involved, and West had never confessed. The older West had also been tight lipped about what he knew and died of a massive heart attack at the funeral home, slumping over in the casket show room.

At the end of the trial, the younger West' innocent pleas fell on deaf ears and the jury was unanimous in its decision to render a guilty verdict---sentenced to life in prison instead of the death penalty. Some people said he'd be up for parole in a few years, that his family would see to it financially, and others said he would never get paroled. Muddy didn't think he would get out early. She certainly hoped not, but she also was suspicious of the deals folks made.

Chapter 5

For the Butterfly People and in memory of the 747 tornado victims from the Tri-State tornado, the highest number of deaths from a single tornado, across the Mississippi River Valley in Illinois, Indiana, and Missouri

1925

When Muddy climbed in bed, the rain had already begun to pelt the tin roof and she could hear the Live Oaks creaking as they swayed in the wind. She knew her yard would be a mess the next morning--magnolia leaves, pine needles and cones, and someone else's trash. It seemed common place for someone else's candy wrapper, plastic bag, or plastic Coke bottle to end up in her yard. She didn't mind cleaning it up, but as she'd become more frail the past couple of years, it was more difficult to stoop or bend to pick up trash. Anthony had fastened some nails close together on the end of an old broomstick when she told him she attempted to pick trash up with the pecan picker upper and it didn't work. She used his homemade invention, and even though she didn't like the flaking yellow paint coming off the old broom handle on her hands, she liked his idea and told him he should patent the idea and market it, despite her feeling people might use them as weapons. Anthony never did make that attempt that she knew of, and this is what she said was a missed opportunity.

It wasn't Anthony's first missed opportunity. His first was going to college. Anthony was smart, could have gone to any college in or out of state, private or public, but he was just one of those birds that didn't want to fly too far away. She had often wondered if it was because he was the first born, because she'd breast fed him too long, or didn't push him to get involved in sports or date. There'd been a girl who really liked Anthony in high school. She'd come from a decent farming family in the country, wore a lot of homemade dresses with patterns Muddy knew had been on sale or discontinued from Woolworth's in Valdosta. When Muddy and one of her friends traveled to Valdosta, they always went to Woolworth's and had a hot dog at the counter. They enjoyed onions and relish on top of the dog, which had been split down the middle and browned on the grill in the back of the store. The dog and a coke were an out of town treat, along with the variety of candy brands at the counter--Bit-O-Honey, Mellocreme (candy corn), caramel creams, and many more.

All three of Muddy's children liked candy, but Anthony was the one who had borderline diabetes that ran on Muddy's daddy's side of the family, and the girl who was sweet on Anthony was a full-fledged diabetic, taking shots from around the time she was ten. It was a shame, really, and Muddy knew this wasn't the reason why Anthony had broken up with her in high school and why he didn't marry her. He was the type of man who would look after a woman and take care of her throughout life. He wasn't the messing around type, and Muddy knew she shouldn't think it, but she wondered if being alone met his needs sexually. In Muddy's day, one didn't talk about such, but Donahue, Oprah, Geraldo, and those sorts of talk shows had certainly opened that area for discussion. Still, Muddy would never openly discuss sexuality with anyone, even her best friends at church. It just wasn't the way Muddy was raised. It was an area that would forever remain discrete for her.

When Anthony broke-up with Tillie Vickers, he didn't sulk around like most, but continued to work hard and study and it seemed to Muddy that he had shut his emotions out completely, which she didn't think was healthy. Tillie, on the other hand, had apparently been devastated, telling people all over town Anthony had dumped her, speculating there might be another girl in whom he was more interested. Of course, Muddy didn't know who Anthony might have dated once he got to Thomasville and on his own, and she never wanted to pry. Occasionally, she might have asked him a question if he first said he'd been to the Rose parade or to a show in Tallahassee: "Who'd you go with to that Willie Nelson concert?" He'd always reply that there were several people who worked at the Piggly Wiggly who went as a group.

Tillie had ended up marrying a farm boy from Brooks County whose daddy's land adjoined her daddy's land. First, they hauled in a single-wide to live in until they could build a small ranch house. Tillie had one child, but the toll on her body was too much with diabetes, and they didn't have additional children. Every once in a while, Muddy would run into Tillie and she was always sweet and asked about Anthony. Muddy didn't like telling Tillie, or anyone else, that Anthony was still single after all these years. She believed people assumed he was a homosexual, that he got around, that he just enjoyed himself, or that he wasn't sexual at all. She could tell what others thought by their half-smiles or raised eyebrows. Muddy'd laugh it off, adding, "I guess I won't get any grandchildren from him." Ultimately, she doesn't care what he was. She would always love him as her son no matter what his choices and regardless of what the Bible said. She knew that it was wrong to disagree, but she felt like her salvation was like an insurance policy and she was covered.

Muddy reached up and turned on the lamp and squinted to grab the phone. "Hello?"

"Mama, you okay?" Anthony asked.

"I was asleep. Why?"

"There's a tornado in Brooks County."

"Where is it?"

"I don't know. News is just playing the alert, showing the map with a red blob in Brooks County. They say it's a fast moving storm."

"What time is it?"

"Around midnight."

"What're you still doing up?"

"A group of us went out to eat late after work and talked."

"What's there to talk about so late?"

"Just life, Mama. No big deal. I'm a grown man."

"I know. I was just asking. Didn't mean to pry. Anyway, it's raining, but I don't even hear wind. I do hear some sirens off in the distance," Muddy said.

"Might've hit somewhere near Morven," Anthony said.

"Well, I'll get up and turn on the TV and if I need you, I'll call you."

"Okay, let me know. I don't mind coming out there if you need me."

"I know. I appreciate it. I'll talk to you later."

Muddy rubbed her eyes, got up, put on her slippers, and headed toward the living room with her cane. She turned on the news out of Tallahassee and there was the map of South Georgia and North Florida, with red blobs all over the place. The screen only showed the map, and a radio voice announced counties under a tornado warning, including Brooks. Muddy heard a bang in the kitchen and felt that kerplunk in her chest, got up, and tried to remember where her pistol was. By the time she was almost to the kitchen, she remembered it was in her chest of drawers underneath a drawer full of belts and scarves. It was wrapped in a handkerchief. She had Claude's old pistols put up in the closet and intended to give those to Lily's boys. Muddy didn't see anything broken in the kitchen and went to the back door, turned on the outside light and opened the wood door. Fortunately, she didn't see anyone, but on the stoop, a bird lay with just a dab of blood on the wood slat. She closed the door and locked it, knowing that if birds were flying at night and into doors, then the tornado must be close. She'd learned long ago to pay attention to animals; they sensed things more than humans. The wind was picking up and the rain was coming down faster and harder and she thought she heard the sound of light hail hitting the roof and porch. Muddy knew the best place to be was in the center of the house, in the bathroom, in the claw foot tub, so she headed down the hall. As she headed down the hall, Muddy heard what she thought was a train, rumbling in the distance, and she'd lived long enough to recognize that as a tornado.

Muddy grabbed the lip of the tub, propped her cane on the wall, pushed her slippers off, stepped in, and sat down. "You'll be fine," she heard Claude whisper, and after a couple of minutes of sitting there, Muddy felt silly. She still heard the roaring sound, but she also thought it was getting more distant. There were certainly high-pitched sounds of wind coming through cracks in window seals, and Muddy made a note that she was probably losing air and heat during the coldest and hottest part of the seasons, causing her power bill to go even higher than the normal increases for bonuses to line the pockets of self-proclaimed, hard-working management who take their families for vacations in the Caribbean instead of nearby beaches in Florida or Georgia or attractions in Orlando. Before the whistling stopped and the wind subsided, Muddy imagined going outside and just throwing up her arms and going with the wind where ever it might take her, like Dorothy in "The Wizard of Oz" except she felt instead of Oz, she might land at the pearly gates and see Claude and her own parents. She also figured if it was her time, she wouldn't even need to go outside; she would simply be gone, flying in a bathtub across Brooks County toward the light. It was a funny image and she told herself she might be going crazy. Not hearing the whistle, wind, or train sound, Muddy gripped the sides of the tub and heaved herself up and out and back into her slippers, and she grabbed the cane. She walked back to the living room, where the TV was still announcing tornados, but Brooks County was no longer on the list. Muddy turned off the television and went on back to bed.

Muddy woke up a little early, trying to recall if all the tornado hoopla was real or a dream, but as she became more conscious, she remembered it more vividly. She crept to the living room and opened the blinds, and there were pinecones and trash everywhere. She sighed. "I just don't think I can get out there and pick it all up," she said to herself. She needed her coffee, walked to the kitchen to prepare a cup, and remembered the bird. She took the broom from the closet, opened the backdoor, and pushed the dead bird off into the hydrangeas. She glanced around the backyard and noted more leaves, some trash, probably from the dumpster at the Suwannee Swifty. Muddy turned and walked back inside to grab the phone.

"Mama, did you have any damage?"

"No, Lily, not that I can tell. I know there was a tornado and I have a lot of debris and trash in the yard, but nothing major."

"They're showing pictures on TV. This whole storm system was awful. Just awful. Alabama and Georgia were hit pretty hard, but so were Missouri and Tennessee. They're reporting a lot of people dead in Missouri."

"That's awful."

"Don't you try to get out there, Mama. I'll get the boys to get over there and pick up your yard for you today."

"Don't be silly. I'm sure that's the last thing they want to do."

"They don't mind one bit. You need anything from Thomasville?"

"I don't think so, but you can call your brothers and tell them that I'm fine, too, so they won't be worried."

"Okay, I'll do that."

Muddy walked back to the living room with her coffee, plopped in the lift chair, and turned on the TV with the remote. She put it first on the local news, which as one might expect, focused more on the local damage. The camera panned a single-wide, which looked as if the Jolly Green giant came running through the woods and kicked it against the trees; the trailer was bent into a horseshow backing into trees, some of which would be forever bent. In the interview, the thick resident shuffled her weight from one leg to the other, like a child needing to go to the restroom and doing her best to hold it; she had teased hair with a comb stuck in it and wore a tank top displaying a portrait of Martin Luther King, Jr. barely covering what some of Muddy's friends would call the woman's hanging baskets because of her missing bra. Muddy thought the woman could have taken the comb out of her hair for the video. "It was terrible." The woman told the reporter. "I heard it coming and knew I was in trouble. I cried and held my children close in that tub and cried to the Lord, and praise Jesus, we safe now." Muddy imagined the woman laid up in her tub to be like a sow, suckling her young. The reporter asked what her family would do now. "We probably stay with my auntie." Muddy was sympathetic to the woman's experience, but felt annoyed by the comb. She felt like her mother should have raised her better.

Muddy turned the channel and they were covering an area in northern Alabama which had been devastated. Fortunately, no one lost life in that tornado, but again several campers had been destroyed that had been set up for a traveling circus. Next to a camper, with images of a bearded lady riding a unicycle, the reporter interviewed a woman who looked identical to the bearded lady minus the beard. She had beady eyes, and while she didn't have a comb stuck in her hair, she was missing several teeth and her fat from her abdomen sagged to just above her knees. She, too, talked about the terror and how she didn't know how the circus people would recover. The screen flashed to images of devastations across the circus grounds: the Ferris wheel on its side and mangled against a fence, wrecked bumper cars piled up, a circus tent was shredded with pieces flapping in the wind. Muddy caught a glimpse of the bearded lady making a slew-footed dash for another camper.

The next scene flashed to middle Tennessee, where only one death had occurred, and it wasn't actually tornado damage, but someone who had a massive heart attack during the tornado. There were two stories, however, that caught Muddy's attention. One was a fellow who'd been for a walk alongside a river and he had grabbed ahold of a tree when he saw the tornado. He commented that at one point he was completely perpendicular to the trunk of the tree; he managed to hang on, screaming out to God for assistance. All trees around him had been uprooted and thrown for hundreds of yards into a subdivision on the other side of the river, through roofs of houses and slamming down on cars in driveways, but the man had managed to hang onto to that lone tree, which was not uprooted. He had received multiple cuts and bruises, but was otherwise fine and quite thankful to see his children. The other story was fascinating, too, but in a different way.

The reporter stood on the concrete slab of what used to be a house; some two-by-fours remained, but were twisted. On one part of the slab, a lone mattress and box spring rested on a wood frame bed. The story was that a boy had come home from school, his parents were at work, and he heard the tornado, ran to his room, and crawled underneath the bed, like he'd been taught. He said he peaked out from under the bed as the room and furniture began to be sucked up into the massive funnel directly over his house, he saw four butterfly people, dressed in flowing robes, and their wings flapped and guided them to his room, where they said, "It's not your time. Do not be afraid. Stay under your bed and we'll protect you." The boy reported he was comforted to the point he fell asleep and only woke later when ambulances, police, and fire truck sirens were blasting in the neighborhood. One emergency medical technician was astonished to see him crawling from underneath the bed and was the first to hear the story. "It's certainly affirming to me," the E.M.T. said. "We've worked scenes where we hear some awesome stories, but this has to be the best one, and if you look, you can't deny the bed was the only thing remaining in the house. Everything else will land in another part of the state," and he was right. It was later reported pictures, checks, and other household belongings came raining down over seventy miles away. The child, of course, wasn't interviewed. He had been taken to the hospital for tests and observation. Muddy was comforted by the story and felt the Lord did indeed work in mysterious ways.

Muddy flipped the channel to CNN where they were covering the damage in Missouri. She was shocked at the devastation, whole areas leveled by the power of spinning wind. Multitudes of people were dead. People looked like zombies walking through the debris, grabbing and holding on to any small piece of their former life—a stuffed animal, a photograph, a knick-knack. One reporter interviewed a family who also mentioned the butterfly people, and this reporter noted that reports of the butterfly people had been documented all the way back to the 1920s. Muddy knew these people weren't butterflies. In fact, she knew they weren't even people, but angels sent to help in a time of need and she was thankful and wondered how people could still not believe and change their ways when the message was clear and blasting all over CNN. The destruction and loss was sad and Muddy shook her head, resolving she would donate money through the Methodist church to help those in need, and she knew there would be many who needed it. What Muddy felt all these scientists should do instead of studying the tornado, chasing them around and taking pictures, and finding new ways to distinguish them as different was figure out a way to stop them. She felt that since tornados were simply a column of rotating air, then something could be done to stop the rotation, like blasting it with air to disperse the other air or having it sucked it into a contraption to slow it or break it up. She imagined it to be like her ceiling fan that she had to turn off and stick something up there to stop it from spinning to change a bulb or flip the switch to reverse its direction with the change of seasons.

While all loss of life was sad to Muddy, the saddest part were the babies—those who hadn't developed, nor had the opportunity to fully live their lives. She imagined they didn't even know they were dying and guessed that they might not be aware they were actually alive, having not established a sense of self. She imagined these were the true angels, and those like them had saved the boy in Tennessee. She knew the babies, and probably most of the children, weren't saved, and while some Christians would maintain they weren't saved and therefore were condemned, she believed this was the epitome of nonsense, narrow-minded, and downright stupid.

In fact, Muddy believed that there were many paths to God, not necessarily one. In fact, she had shared that one day in her Sunday School class. Most of the members had a quizzical look, heads cocked to one side. One of the members told how an aunt of hers began to stray from her core beliefs late in life and say crazy things and it turned out she had hardening of the arteries and was oxygen deprived. Some still had a quizzical look because they weren't clear how that story related, but Muddy got it. She knew the old woman was telling the story as an analogy to let Muddy know how the old woman felt about Muddy's idea, but Muddy just smiled at her and said, "We'll see." Muddy could see the fear of death in the old woman's eyes and there was a nervous cough and shift, the old woman tugging at her skirt, exhibiting her own discomfort at Muddy's remark.

Chapter 6

In memory of the Alday family
victims of Georgia's worst mass murder in 1973

While she was cooking eggs and frying bacon, Muddy heard the tires spit pea gravel in the driveway when Todd's Camaro skidded to a stop. She pulled the curtain and peaked out the kitchen window and noted that Tom was with Todd. Muddy preferred ancestral names, like her own Charlotte, and like those she'd assigned her children when they were born. She didn't know where Sid and Lily had come up with Todd and Tom for names, but she'd inquired of Lily when the second grandchild Tom was born: "Well, why did you have to give Tom a T name like Todd?" Lily'd responded, "I don't know, Mama. I like T's." Muddy thought Lily had been more of a parallel, linear type thinker and liver of life, and she was, but she'd always wanted to be different, tried to be different, experimented with a more perpendicular or T-life. One of her favorite movies was "Easy Rider" with Peter Fonda. In fact, Lily had even dated a boy with a motorcycle who'd gone by Thor. Muddy'd wondered if Lily hadn't named her boys T names because of Thor. That relationship didn't work out, and Muddy was glad. Riding on the back of a motorcycle didn't appeal to Muddy, and she'd lay awake at night worrying about Lily. About a year after that relationship ended, Thor had been killed on his motorcycle, going too fast and running under a semi, lopping off his head, helmet included, where it rolled from I-75 up the embankment and into the parking lot of a rest area. The would be good Samaritan who apparently went to pick it up didn't know a head was in it and dropped it, went running and screaming to the custodian on the premises who called 911. Lily never dated nor rode another motorcycle that Muddy knew of and neither did her boys, and Muddy made a mental note to tell Todd and Tom the story, so maybe they wouldn't ride one either. She thought she'd keep the name Thor to herself.

Lily's outsider experiments never took. Muddy saw Lily's naming of her children T names as symbolic and she thought her daughter probably hoped the children would be renegades, but Muddy also knew that if Lily was honest with herself, she wouldn't want that for her children. No mother wants that, Muddy believed. Once Lily got engaged to Sid, Muddy finally felt a peace come over her she hadn't felt since before Lily entered puberty. Sid was solid and while Muddy knew he wasn't a risk taker and they'd probably never have much more than she and Claude had, she didn't care. She wanted her to be happy and settle down and accept the hand she'd been dealt. Todd and Tom were going to be Lily's cross to bear. Both were fairly good-looking boys and both had been active in sports activities and were currently playing baseball in high school. Todd was eighteen and in the twelfth grade, and Tom was fifteen and in the ninth grade. Todd was the better-looking one, though Muddy knew she shouldn't think it and certainly should never say it, but his problem was that he knew he was good looking and didn't mind saying it. He was sarcastic and a rule breaker, knowing enough about rules to know what he could get away with and what he couldn't. In that sense, Muddy felt like he was like Timothy. Tom, on the other hand, was more plain-looking, but Muddy felt in the long run, he would be the better looking one. He had some acne that Muddy thought might scar his face, but she also knew a good personality and charm could cover up anything from a limp to baldness and certainly would trump pot holes from acne.

Muddy knew they didn't want to be at her house cleaning up the yard, really. Like Lily, once they'd begun to go through puberty, they'd become even more focused on themselves. The hormonal changes don't make for nice boys who love and want to spent time with their grandmother. In South Georgia, hormonal changes made for bullying at school, smoking and drinking, smashing mailboxes along country roads on the weekend. Hormones certainly didn't make for church-going and hymn-singing, but if teenage boys got jobs, then most of their energy went into hard work. Work had saved many boys from ending up in trouble.

Muddy remembered Claude had been a bit on the wild side in his younger days, too. She knew that is where Lily had got it from, but then, Muddy also knew there was a part of her that enjoyed it. She remembered clearly how passionate Claude had been when they were dating and even when they were first married, before the children. She remembered vividly his advances when they were alone: in their car, on the beach, and even in the kitchen before she'd made the curtains. She could remember it with such clarity that she became excited and quickly deposited the memories back into the bank where they could be withdrawn at night when she was alone and desired comfort.

Todd knocked, and Muddy regained her composure and hollered, "You boys come on in. I'm cooking you some breakfast."

"Smells good," Todd said.

"Sure does," Tom followed.

"I know good and well your mama don't cook you boys bacon and eggs. Never did, but before you get out there and clean up, you need some energy." The boys smiled.

"I know your mama also told you not to take money, but my plan is to give you both some. You can use it for something. Just don't tell her."

"Thanks, grandma," said Tom.

"You're welcome. I'm just glad to see ya'll. I never get to see ya'll anymore. Ya'll are getting to be men and too busy with girls to worry about your old Grandma."

They giggled, but they didn't refute what Muddy'd said, so she felt a bit annoyed. She wanted them to regret it, apologize for not coming more often, and tell her they loved her. After they cleaned their plates, they headed out, dragging the powder blue Morven trash cans around the yard and filling them until all debris was cleared. She was nodding off in the chair with the news playing when the back screen door slammed and Todd and Tom let her know they were finished.

"Thank ya'll," she said. She handed them a twenty each, and they told her they appreciated it. She grabbed her cane, got up, and started to the kitchen. "Sit down and let me get ya'll some tea. Cool off a bit before going." Todd and Tom sat on the sofa and watched the news. Muddy returned with iced tea and perked up at the headlines. She didn't even hear Tom telling her thanks for the tea. The anchor reported that Carl Isaacs, the longest serving death row inmate, almost thirty years, the ringleader in the murder of the Alday family, one of the worst mass murders in the history of Georgia, had finally been put to death in a Pennsylvania prison by lethal injection. As a refresher for viewers who would likely not recall details after thirty years, the reported revealed that Isaacs and two others had escaped a Maryland prison, picked up Isaacs' half-brother in Pennsylvania, where they stole a car, killed the driver, and made their way to Seminole County, Georgia where they robbed and shot members of the Jerry Alday family. They had taken Mr. Alday's wife hostage, brutally raping, shooting, and leaving her body in the woods to be discovered days later. The four were discovered in West Virginia several days later and were arrested, tried, and found guilty. Muddy remembered it clearly, and she had a clipping of this in a shoebox. She thought she'd pull it and reread it later.

All three were glued to the story, to the review from the 1970s.

"Did you see those clothes?" Todd asked.

"Yeah," said Tom.

"That was the style," said Muddy. "I was glad to see the 70s go."

"Wonder why they kept that guy on death row so long?" Todd asked.

"Who knows," said Muddy. "They should have killed him a long time ago. All he was doing was sitting up there costing taxpayers money." She felt herself getting upset, felt her face getting hot, and knew her ears were probably red. Claude always made fun of her for that; he didn't seem to get upset about much of anything, which is why Muddy believed he'd fallen over dead one day on the lawn mower--holding all that emotion inside and stressing his body.

"Isn't that against Christianity?" Todd asked.

"I don't think so," Muddy said, "but if it is, then that's fine, too."

Todd didn't respond, but Tom said, "Preacher told us the death penalty is wrong."

"Well, every preacher has a different view on this, but never put your faith in a preacher." The boys didn't say anything and Muddy added, "There's so much killing and death, and at my age, that's just about all I see. You boys are young and need to live and enjoy life. Time passes and we are passing with it and seems like the older you get, the faster it goes. Ya'll want some more tea?"

"No mam," they both responded.

"Come back here with me. I've got something I want to give ya'll." They went into one of the spare bedrooms, and Muddy opened the closet door, flipped the light switch. The closet reeked of moth balls, and she noticed Todd and Tom turning up their noses. She pulled the wire hangers holding clothing across the wooden rod and stopped, thumbing through them to see what was what. She pulled out two coats and two vests. "These were your granddaddy's and I think ya'll can finally wear them. Try them on. They're Barbour from England and cost a small fortune." She could tell by the looks on their faces they were excited.

"Grandma, these are great," Todd said. "These will look great on me."

"Yeah," said Tom. "I appreciate it."

"He would've wanted ya'll to have them. I've got something else for you, too."

She grabbed a wooden box from one of the built-in side shelves and brought it to the bed. She opened it and inside were a couple of pistols and some medals. "These medals your granddaddy earned when he was in the Guard. He was never deployed, except in Georgia in the 1960s when racial tension rose after Martin Luther King, Jr. was shot. These guns he purchased early on when he was still interested in shooting. I think he picked off many a squirrel in the trees out back. Of course, that was before the town passed an anti-shooting ordinance. Course, that don't matter on Saturday night when people get drunk."

The boys chuckled.

"Make sure they aren't loaded and be careful with them at home. I also don't won't you boys riding motorcycles. You hear me?"

Before they could respond, or Muddy could elaborate on Thor's head, Tom opened his and spun the cylinder and it was clear, but Todd didn't check. He looked down the barrel and pulled the trigger over and over; the last click was quick and it seemed as if time froze as the explosion sent the bullet whizzing right past Muddy's ear, shattering the old single pane glass and shattering the plate glass window across the street while half-deaf Fred Stalvey sat on the toilet, frustrated and constipated and reading an antique car magazine he'd picked up when he bought his lotto ticket at the Suwannee Swifty. He wanted to check and see if the value of his antique, convertible Thunderbird had gone up since the last time he checked. Of course, it would have been cheaper, quicker, and easier to search the internet, but he didn't know how. The house shook from the glass shattering and Stalvey heard something and felt the vibration in his feet. While trying to stand up, he slipped and bumped his head on the window seal and fell unconscious to the linoleum floor.

"Oh my God," Muddy said. "Shit!"

The boys said nothing, partly in shock at the seriousness of Todd's action and partly in shock at hearing their grandmother saying "shit," something they had no idea was possible. Muddy was embarrassed she used a four letter word in front of her grandchildren and regretted it, not because she'd used it, but because she'd lost control and it just slipped out. Within seconds, a lone siren could be heard getting closer. Muddy wasn't worried about her window. She was worried if the trajectory of the bullet had gone to Stalvey's house. "God forbid you hit that old Thunderbird of his. He'll kill us. The ass." Muddy craned her next to see, but the thick Magnolia blocked her view.

"I'm sorry, Grandma," Todd said.

"It'll work out," she said.

They had moved to the porch by the time the patrol car pulled into the driveway. Sgt. Turner wasn't running, but the tall, lanky policeman was moving quickly. There was no sign of Stalvey, but his truck was in his driveway, the Thuderbird apparently tucked away in the single car garage attached to the walkway leading to his back door.

"Ya'll okay?"

"I'm so sorry. I was giving my grandsons these guns and one went off and went through the front bedroom window," Muddy explained. "It was an accident."

"That's fine, Ms. Rewis. Do you know if it hit anything else?"

"If it did, it went to Stalvey's. He's not over here yet, so that makes me worry."

The boys walked into the front yard, Muddy sat in the swing and kept looking toward Stalvey's house, and Sgt. Turner rang Stalvey's bell and knocked. He noticed the plate glass window missing, zig-zag pieces of glass dangling from wood and he could see and hear the poodle running to and from the hallway, where Turner could make out a foot sticking out of the bathroom door. He took a credit card from his wallet and jimmied the front lock and opened the door.

"Mr. Stalvey, you okay?" The Sgt. didn't get a response, pressed the shoulder microphone, asking for back-up and an ambulance. "We have a potential gunshot victim here."

"Who is it?" the dispatcher asked.

"Fred Stalvey. 311 North Church Street. Apparently Ms. Rewis discharged a firearm by accident and it went through his window."

"Lord, it'll take a few minutes to get here from Hahira."

"Mr. Stalvey," Turner called, touching his foot and trying to turn him over to see if he was shot. He managed to get down in the floor and noted blood.

"Hey, what's going on here?" Stalvey opened his eyes, blinking hard as if to clear night matter.

"Have you been shot?"

"Shot?"

"Yes, sir, Mrs. Rewis apparently shot out your living room window."

"Why in the hell would she do that?"

"Sir, I think it was an accident."

"I don't think I was shot. Last thing I remember I was looking at this magazine and trying to take a shit. I must have slipped and hit my head."

"See if you can sit up," the Sgt. said. "I've got an ambulance on the way."

"I don't need no damned ambulance. I'm fine." As Stalvey tried to stand and pull up his pants, he became light-headed and fell back against the wall.

"Come on, now, hold on to me and I'll get you in here to a chair." Sgt. held him under his arms, guided him to the living room to a chair on the opposite side of the room. He could see the missing window, the glass on his sofa and wood floor. Prissy, the poodle, continued to prance around bark, yap and nip at the officer's heels. "Shut the hell up, Prissy," Stalvey said, raising his hand. Prissy made her whiney sound and tapped through the house and into the kitchen. Stalvey could see Muddy sitting in the swing, her grandsons in the yard, all of them cupping their hands over their foreheads to block the sun and see. Sgt. Turner returned from the kitchen with a wet paper towel and placed it on the cut just above Stalvey's brow.

"Just hold this on there, and it'll stop bleeding in a minute. Keep your head back."

"It'll probably bleed a while. I take blood thinner." Stalvey leaned his head back.

Turner noticed cars driving up and down Church Street. Several people were standing on the curb by the Suwannee Swifty and the General Dollar store seeing what they could see, and of course, since Sgt. Turner had not talked in code, as he had been taught at the Police Academy at the college in Tifton, folks in Morven and Brooks County had heard the comments over the police scanner, and several who knew Stalvey and Rewis made calls to others. Within ten minutes, Sunday School members were calling Muddy. She tried to rush them off the phone, assuring everyone she was fine, but the last caller angered her and turned her ears red.

"Hello?"

"Muddy, honey, how you?"

Muddy recognized the voice immediately. It was Velma Anderson, the worst gossip in Brooks County. Muddy despised her, as did several people. In fact, she didn't have any friends that Muddy knew of, just plenty of relatives who weren't much better Velma. "I'm fine."

"Well, I heard you've had a busy day."

"Yes, but we're all fine now."

"Well, you hadn't been sharing with us at church."

"What do you mean?"

"I didn't know about Mr. Stalvey."

"Apparently, he'll be fine."

"I mean, you and Mr. Stalvey."

"What are you talking about, Velma?"

"They said over the police radio he was naked and you shot him in his own house. I didn't know ya'll had something going on."

Muddy felt the kerplunk, but she didn't know if it was because she was so annoyed with Velma or if it was the thought of Todd of shooting Mr. Stalvey. "I don't have anything going on with that old man," Muddy said. I was giving my grandsons Claude's pistols, and one of them accidentally shot out his window. I don't know if he's been shot or not. I know we shot out his window. I hope he'll be okay."

"Me, too," said Velma.

"Thanks for calling," Muddy said, turning off the phone and not waiting for a goodbye response from Velma. "Damn woman," she said to herself. The boys were still in the yard and occasionally telling passersby who had their car windows down what happened if they asked. While the Emergency

Medical Technicians were dealing with Mr. Stalvey, Sgt. Turner had jogged back across the road to let Mrs. Rewis and her grandsons know that Stalvey was fine, but the gun shot and window breaking noises had apparently startled him and he'd slipped off the toilet and hit his head. Muddy found some humor in the situation. Sgt. Turner said he understood it was an accident and asked if Mrs. Rewis would agree to replace Mr. Stalvey's window. Muddy nodded.

"Then, I think we can consider this incident over. He's fairly cantankerous and refuses to go to the hospital. "

"And they'll be glad he didn't, but I'll never hear the end of this. Lord have mercy."

When Sgt. Turner was gone, and the boys finally left with their new toys, Muddy made a tomato sandwich and watched a little news. She began to nod a little in her chair when the phone rang. She knew it was Lily. It had only been about thirty minutes since the boys had left, and she knew they would have run right in the house to show their mother the new toys. Muddy knew Lily would be upset when she answered.

"Mama, what in the world did you do?"

"Your daddy would have wanted it this way and I don't want to hear no more about it."

"Okay, fine, Mama. Have you talked with Mr. Stalvey?"

"No."

"You ought to go over there and tell him you're sorry."

"I'm not going over there. There're enough rumors now."

"What do you mean?"

"Oh, never mind. I'll call him later."

"Maybe you could cook him a pie or something."

"I'm not cooking him a pie. I'm paying for a new window."

"Mama, you could be a bit nicer. After all, he was daddy's friend."

"Yes, he was. Your daddy's friend. He's an ass."

"Mama, such talk from a devout Methodist."

"The Lord would agree," Muddy said. "I've got to go. Someone's at the door." No one was at the door, but Muddy believed in little white lies that never grew and often it was for the other person's own good. She was tired.

Chapter 7

In memory of the victims of Northwest Flight 255 (where 154 victims died and one child, Cecelia Cichan, was the lone survivor), August, 1987

Muddy wouldn't have answered the phone if she didn't have caller I.D. and she rolled her eyes when she saw it was Timothy. She knew Lily had called him and stirred him up, too, but like Todd, Timothy would have shot out the window, too, if he had been afforded such an opportunity when he was a teen.

"Hello?"

"You okay, Mama? Do I need to come over there?"

"I don't mind you coming over here, but no, you don't need to."

"You know what I mean. Did you get fined or did Mr. Stalvey harass you?"

"Certainly not, nor would I have accepted a fine or his harassment."

"Well, good. Lily's not too happy with you for giving her boys those guns."

"She'll get over it."

"Mama, I know you've had a rough day, but do you think that was the best decision to make?"

"Look here, I make the best decisions I can, and it's not your place to question me. You call me back when you have a better disposition." Muddy turned off the phone, sat it on its holder, and unplugged the phone. She'd had enough of the phone for the day. She poured herself some more tea and took a long swig. She normally didn't cut Timothy off, or anyone else for that matter, but she was rattled. She needed to rest, relax. She walked back to the bedroom, turned on the ceiling fan, put the tea glass on the night stand, kicked off her flats, and laid down, covering up with her old quilt. Before she could reach over to the night stand and take another swig of tea, she was out. Muddy awoke to the sound of the doorbell ringing over and over and sat up, confused. She looked at the clock and it was midafternoon. She took a swig of tea and made her way to the front door, peaking out to see it was Stalvey. She wasn't in the mood for him.

"Charlotte, you in there?"

Muddy opened the door. "I was laying down."

"I didn't mean to wake you."

"You didn't. I was just resting. All these events today have worn me out, and for your window and troubles, I apologize. I had hoped to get to tell you in person. I'll be glad to pay for it."

"Thank you, but the officer said he thought one of your grandsons probably did it and you were covering for them."

"What does it matter?" Muddy always had a way of side-stepping anything she didn't want to discuss.

"I reckon it don't matter."

"How's your head?" Muddy could see the bandage and tape.

"It's finally eased off a bit." He touched his forehead, and just as he did, a new trickle of blood rolled down his cheek.

"Oh my, you're bleeding. Come on in and let me get you a wet paper towel."

Muddy unlatched the door and Mr. Stalvey came in and glanced around. "Hadn't been in here in a long time," he said.

"I know," said Muddy. "Sit down and make yourself at home. I won't be a minute. You want some tea?"

"Would love some," Stalvey said, and he wasn't being polite. He'd been drinking instant tea since his wife was killed in a plane crash. She'd been the one to make tea daily, and Stalvey simply couldn't get it like hers. He missed Charlene. She'd been a teacher at the Morven Elementary school for many years and when summer came, she always looked forward to visiting her sister in Arizona for a couple of weeks. Charlene's sister would take her around, and they would collect all sorts of things to bring back to Morven to show the children, especially Native American artifacts. Fred remembered the morning clearly. She was frantically scrambling around the house, labeling things in the kitchen for him. She'd put three casseroles in the fridge with labels, so he wouldn't go hungry for two weeks. She figured he would get at least three meals each from casseroles, and she had even cooked a ham and sliced it, so he'd have sandwiches. She'd even made two gallons of tea. She drove her Chrysler LeBaron over to Valdosta, where she parked and boarded the puddle jumper to Atlanta. From Atlanta, she had flown to Detroit to change planes for Phoenix. The weather was clear, so Fred wasn't worried a bit and had gone on about his day, as usual. Late in the afternoon, Evelyn, Charlene's sister, called in a panic, wanting to know what plane Charlene was on because there had been a bad crash. Fred didn't know.

Fred had scrambled around the kitchen and bedroom, where they kept papers. He was worried about it, but saw no reason to get emotional and kept telling himself that Evelyn was over reacting. After talking with Fred, Evelyn had gone to the airport and checked the flight records and verified Charlene was on the flight, and she called Fred back with the bad news. For a day or two, Fred, Evelyn, and everyone else didn't really know what to do. Charlene's body was not recovered. It took Fred months before he had any sort of semblance of normality. In fact, it had been years, and he still didn't understand. One moment she was there and the next moment she was simply gone.

Most had been killed in the explosion, as the plane rolled left, hit an electric pole that severed the wing, and fell onto the interstate, but some bodies were recovered and there was a lone survivor, a four year old girl who had been held by her mother. While the girl was burned, had several broken bones, she had somehow survived the accident, which was blamed on the pilots. Several years after the crash, someone from the airline had contacted Fred to let him know about a monument that was being erected in Detroit and a ceremony that would occur, but Fred told them he couldn't travel that far. He had erected his own monument to remember Charlene in the newer portion of the cemetery at First Baptist. He'd had a memorial service for Charlene at First Baptist, too, and many of her former elementary students had come. It had broken Muddy's heart and she had clipped the article in the newspaper to save.

"This tea sure is good, Charlotte."

"Why thank you, Fred."

"You're welcome. Your tea is better than Charlene's was."

Muddy laughed. "I still miss Charlene and think about her."

"Yeah, I think about her, too, almost every day. And I think about Claude. I miss him. Miss our fishing together."

"I know you do and I miss him, too."

"He used to talk about you mostly on our fishing trips," Fred revealed.

"Me? I thought ya'll talked about men stuff---politics and sports."

"We did, but we talked about lots of stuff."

"Like what?"

"You know that memorial they put up for that woman who was lynched back in the 1900s?"

"Yes, I know about that. Her name was Mary Turner. My grandson Todd is friends with a descendent of Mary Turner. Her name is Shaneka Harris. I went to the marker service with Lily."

"He'd be glad ya'll went. His Mama's granddaddy was one of the men who helped do it. So was mine."

"You're not serious?"

"Yes, I am."

"Oh, dear Lord. Why didn't he ever tell me about that?"

"I think he wanted to, Charlotte. I think he felt like you'd think less of him somehow, as if the sins of ancestors transfer."

"That's ridiculous."

"I agree. I told him there was nothing we could do about it that would undo the pain and suffering she felt. We have to move on, to learn from our mistakes."

"That's right, but maybe there's something we could do," Muddy said.

"What?"

"Let's set up a scholarship in Mary Turner's memory. Between the two of us, we could afford it, and it would help educate others about her story."

"That's a good idea. Of course, your children might not like you spending their inheritance. And since Charlene and I never had children, I guess most of mine will go to nieces and nephews I don't hear from, or the church. I wished we would have been able to have children. We tried to adopt a boy here, but they wouldn't hear of it because of Charlene's depression."

"I didn't know Charlene had depression. She never talked about it."

"You know, back then people didn't talk about it. You know she'd tried to kill herself and was hospitalized. Slit her wrists and I found her in the tub. This was a few years after we were married and before we lived here. But it was in her records and they didn't like it because she was taking medication for it and did all the years we were married. I think her being a school teacher helped, but she was trying to save that boy from being sent off. Charlene always said she had plenty of children: she had them all day at school, but didn't have to worry about bathing, feeding or clothing them, and then she had me."

Muddy laughed. "That's right."

"I do wished we could have adopted that boy before he got sent off to the Florida School for the Boys. I appealed and appealed thinking they'd give in and let us have him, and we finally gave up the idea."

"Was it the Hank Holloway boy?"

"Yeah, that's right. Hank Holloway. Charlene had him in class, but it was Claude who said he'd been sent away and had written to ya'll and wanted to come back and live here. He tried to get us to adopt him. Said he'd thought about it himself, but just didn't think ya'll could take on another mouth to feed."

"Lord have mercy. All this time, I blamed myself for not reading that letter and Claude had read it and tried to do something."

"Why would you blame yourself?"

"Well, that school abused them boys. Some died there and are buried in unmarked graves. I found the letter just this week and had Timothy check on Hank. He was never discharged in the records, but there was no record of him dying either."

"Oh, that's awful."

"Yes, it is."

"You assume he died, then?"

"That or he ran off somewhere."

"Maybe he did. I sure hope so."

"Me, too, but it would have been tough on him in the world all alone. That's why I gave my grandsons those pistols. I want them to protect themselves, their families, but even more I wanted them to remember Claude. After a while, it's like he was never here, like I'm not here, like no one before us was here."

"I know what you mean."

"You know, I've never messed with those guns and wouldn't have either if I'd known one was loaded. To tell you the truth, when Todd pulled that trigger, I thought he'd shot me. I nearly fell to the floor. I think if I'd been standing six inches to the right, I'd be in the funeral home this afternoon."

"Well, I'm glad he didn't shoot you, but at least now I know who the shooter was."

Muddy laughed. "Well, I guess I let that slip, didn't I?"

"Yep."

"How long has Charlene been gone now?"

"Well, it's been several years. It was 1987."

"Goodness. The investigation showed pilot error in that crash. You think someone pays for that, Fred? I mean, do you think the pilot is a murderer?"

"I've thought about that. I don't think so. I don't think it was intentional on his part. You know, his family suffered a loss, too. That's why I never sued. I think some of the families sued, but it won't bring back their family members and money won't help them fill that emptiness. There's just too many lawsuits these days."

"I think you're right about that."

"I better be going," he said.

"Yeah, or we'll have old Velma Anderson stirring something up."

"Velma Anderson?"

"Oh, she's just an old nosey gossip. She's already called here today having heard this and that so she said."

"That woman is nuts. She all but threw herself at me when Charlene died. Called, brought stuff by, checked on me, even after everyone else had quit checking, she kept on. I finally figured it out and had to run her off."

"Ha! That's funny."

"Not to me it wasn't," Fred said.

"I guess not. Well, I appreciate you coming over, but more importantly, I appreciate you sharing those stories with me."

"Anytime," Fred said.

They walked onto the front porch and Muddy sat in the swing. As Fred was making his way down the steps, it occurred to Muddy that Fred wasn't as bad as she had built him up to be these years and certainly not what her perception had been. He had been pleasant, not the womanizer she imagined. He had shown good manners, not the rude, know-it-all she thought. Most of all, he had talked with her, not at her, being respectful and sharing important information that made her feel better and more complete than she had in a long time.

"Fred, you let me know how much the window is and I'll write you a check."

"Glass guy is coming tomorrow. I'll get you an estimate."

"Alright."

They said goodbye, and off Fred walked in basically the same path the bullet had taken. Muddy leaned back in the swing, rubbing her feet together, feeling better than she'd felt in years. She wondered about the Mary Turner story and if she should tell the children the truth. She wondered if it would make a difference in their lives. If Shaneka knew, then she probably wouldn't be friends with Todd, but Muddy didn't want to get involved in their business and decided she wouldn't be the one to tell it. She didn't think it made much of a difference to her, and she wondered if Claude met Mary in heaven and what he said. She didn't think Claude's ancestor would be in heaven. She wondered about Hank Holloway, whether he was dead or alive, and if he was alive, what became of him. It was always interesting to Muddy to see children and how they turned out. Fat children become thin, and thin children become fat. Smart children do not apply themselves and dumb children apply themselves and become successful. It was a mixed bag. Life reminded her of a harbor in Maine she'd once seen on a bus trip she and Claude had taken with a group of seniors. The harbor had been full of sail boats, all different sizes and shapes and sails so colorful that it truly looked like a postcard one would send friends and family back home. It was beautiful. When she looked at friends and family, she didn't see positive and negative; she saw variety and every one of them were equally beautiful. It reminded her of a song by Andy Williams and she began to hum it while the swing swayed back and forth, the chain creaking on the hooks in the ceiling.

Chapter 8

In memory of the 909 victims of the Jonestown mass suicide, 1978

When Muddy heard the phone ringing, she figured it would be Lily calling and raising cane again that she had given the boys Claude's guns, but it wasn't. It was Anthony calling with bad news he'd learned.

"Mama, have you heard about Clara?"

"No, what happened?"

"She died last night."

"Oh, Lord. Heart attack?" Both Clara's parents, Claude's brother and his wife, had died suddenly from massive heart attacks, too, over in Thomasville.

"No, they think it might've been an overdose."

"What?"

"An overdose," he said louder.

"I heard you. I'm just surprised."

"They found two empty pill bottles on her coffee table. She was on the sofa, her arms folded on her chest as if she were already in her coffin. Left a note and funeral instructions."

"Who found her?"

"Her neighbor went over when the porch light wasn't turned off by mid-morning and she couldn't get her on the phone. Told the police she felt weird about peaking in the front window, but could see her laying there. I stopped by when I heard and she saw me pull in and came over to tell me the same story. Do you know she even asked about her porch furniture and flowers?"

"Clara ain't in the ground and the neighbor is wanting her stuff. That beats all. Oh, I just can't believe it. Bless Clara's heart. Do you know when the visitation and funeral will be?"

"No, I know it'll be at Allen and Allen downtown by the hospital, but I don't know about the funeral. If she committed suicide, will they have one at her church?"

"Well, why wouldn't they?"

"Because she killed herself."

"Well, first, they don't really know that, do they? They're making assumptions. Anyway, the funeral is for the living, and whether they agree with her killing herself, if she did it or not, it's not up to the preacher or the church to judge her. If she did, wonder why she would have done something like that?"

"I don't know, Mama. Last time I saw her in the grocery store, she told me she was taking some new medication which made her feel better. She looked better than she had in a while. I didn't know she had been suffering from depression again."

"Oh yeah, she's had depression for years and I think had taken medicine for it ever since that Promat came out and made big news. I think there were some people taking it just to feel better even if they weren't depressed."

"You mean, Prozac?"

"That's right. I think Clara's mama had it bad, too, but she never took anything that I know of, but when we did go visit them, I always took her something--pecans from our trees, something from our garden, or roses from my flower beds. It always cheered her up and her disposition was better. Just something little makes a difference."

"I'll let you know more when I can find out."

"Did you tell your brother and sister?"

"No, but I'll let them know."

"Alright, call me and let me know. I'll try to get over there for the visitation and funeral. You want to ride to Marianna one day this week? Maybe after Clara's service? I want to see what I can find out about that Holloway boy."

"Yeah, I could do that."

Once they hung up, Muddy thought she should have told Anthony about the gunshot and broken window, so he wouldn't be worried about it, but he was what she called a "worry wart" and it didn't matter how positive a spin she put on the story, he would worry. Anthony would come fix her window when he found out. In the meantime, she stuck some cardboard from a box she had saved in the closet in the frame that was missing and didn't think it mattered much anyway. She was more worried about mosquitoes getting in the house than robbers or rapists at this point. She didn't think now that it was all over town she'd shot at Mr. Stalvey anyone would be messing with her.

Muddy thought about Clara, lying on the sofa, her hands folded across her chest. She didn't understand depression or suicide. She remembered clearly the mass suicide in Jonestown, Guyana, seeing all those bodies so still and neat next to each other from drinking Flavor Aid mixed with cyanide. Some had said it was mass murder, but to Muddy, suicide was murder, too, just depending on who did the act—the person who died or someone else. She believed people had come to some thinking in their mind which was somehow corrupted, but once someone was convinced, it was hard to get them to back down from the belief. This was true in Jonestown, and she had saved the article she found it so odd. It was also true with an even stranger, and more recent, mass suicide called Heaven's Gate, where the group thought they would join a UFO trailing behind a comet, and it was true with Clara. Muddy hoped the good Lord forgave her.

Muddy was glad Anthony would call Lily and Timothy, and Muddy knew Lily would take care of the flowers from their family. Muddy had asked her to take that practice over when the florist in Morven died and the shop closed. Muddy didn't want a new account in Thomasville or anywhere else, and she didn't want to establish a new relationship with a florist. She knew to give Lily her share of the cost, as did the brothers.

She'd liked Morven's florist Big Al, which is what everyone called him. When he'd opened the shop in the 1960s, he had a wonderful personality, dressed nice, and was very complimentary to all the women, making comments on shoes, handbags, hair, and what-not, and through the years, he continued his tradition, but he had become sickly at some point and took a lot of medication. Some said he had cancer, some said he had cirrhosis, and some said he had AIDS. Muddy never asked. It didn't matter to her what he had or how he got it. She knew he was prone to drink, probably was homosexual, and might have cancer, but what mattered to her was that he didn't suffer. So, she popped in and took him pies, pecans, or some vegetables from her garden, not so much because she wanted him to gain weight, but because she believed the visit and gesture was good for a sick soul, and he always smiled and was pleased to see her and appreciative of her gesture. Muddy remembered Claude saying, "You didn't get too close to him, did you?" Muddy had laughed and said, "You can catch what he's got by sitting next to him and holding his hand while he's dying." He'd told her he didn't know why she was going over there so much, that it wasn't like they were kin, to which she'd replied, "He's been a part of this family and community for years and has helped us with everything you can imagine: Lily's wedding, Timothy's wedding, my parents funerals, your parents funerals, church luncheons, pageants at school and church, you name it. Just because he was a Yankee and probably a homosexual, you want him to just lay up there in that house and die alone? No one really deserves that, Claude. Maybe you should go with me." She remembered Claude spinning on his heels and heading outside, never to mention Al again, though he did attend the small service at the Methodist church with her. Several of Al's friends were there and they were dispersed in the congregation. After he was buried, an attorney from Valdosta approached the minister, and word got around quickly that Al had visited with the minister, become a Christian, and had left his house to the church, his florist inventory to a friend in Thomasville, and a few thousand dollars in the bank to another friend up north who never bothered to come to the funeral. Of course, Muddy believed people should come to a funeral out of respect and appreciation to the deceased, not because something had been left for the living.

Life was quiet for Muddy the next couple of days, and she found a bill in her mailbox from a glass company and assumed Stalvey had put it in there because it wasn't in an envelope—something Muddy recalled someone from her Sunday School class saying she'd been told by the Post Office she shouldn't put things in mailboxes that didn't go through the Postal Service. Muddy thought it was silly if it was true. After all, it wasn't really the Post Office's mailbox. Plus, she knew plenty of rules they broke themselves and had seen it on television—mail delivered wrong, mail took home with the postman instead of returning it to the Post Office, and so on. Like most government workers, Muddy figured they created rules to insure job security. She had heard about the good benefits and retirement; like legislators, their benefits were better than the benefits of most Americans and yet, the taxpayers were paying for them. It was enough to make her sick.

Muddy paid her bills the first of the month after her Social Security and retirement deposits were there. There weren't many bills—power, water and sewer, garbage, and cable. Insurance and taxes Muddy paid quarterly, but she wrote a check to Stalvey and addressed the envelope, mailing it at the Post Office along with her other bills. She even wrote Stalvey a brief note that she appreciated his cooperation and was very sorry for the unfortunate event. On Thursday afternoon, the doorbell rang and Muddy found Stalvey at the door. He told her he just wanted to thank her for her promptness in sending him the check.

"I don't like to wait too long," Muddy told him. "I might forget."

"Me, too."

"You want a glass of tea?"

"Sure," he said, walking in and filling the living room with a scent Muddy recognized: Bruit. For a moment, she glanced about the room, hoping to see a vision of Claude and figured it must be Fred Stalvey wearing the cologne.

When she was walking back in the living room, she thought he looked distressed. "Is something the matter?"

"Yes," he said.

"What is it?"

"Me."

"What do you mean? Are you sick?"

"No, I'm nervous."

"Why? Is someone out there?"

"No, it's someone in here."

"What? Who?" Muddy became frantic and began to look about her room, as if someone would jump out from behind the sofa, and wondering if he could see Claude.

"Who? I mean me."

"Oh," she said.

As she moved forward to hand off the glass, he said, "I'll just get to the point. Would you like go out?"

Muddy spilled the tea on his shirt and moved as quickly as she could back to the kitchen. "I'm so sorry. Let me get some damp paper towels. When she began dabbing them onto his chest, Mr. Stalvey lost his balance and fell backward onto the sofa, and Muddy went tumbling with him to the sofa. It happened so fast, that all Muddy could say was, "Lord." They were face to face, her on top of him, and he was giggling, and she was scrambling to get up and couldn't use her arms to lift herself.

"I'm so sorry," he said. "But I'm not nervous anymore. Here, let me help you." He reached his right arm to her backside, to get a good enough grip to turn her toward the floor, but his grip on her buttocks alarmed Muddy. "Get your hand off me."

"Oh," he said. "I didn't mean to."

"Fred Stalvey, I don't appreciate your getting fresh with me. Help me up."

"I was trying," he said.

When she was finally on the floor, Lily appeared in the doorway, which had been left open. "What is going on here?"

"Damn," Muddy said.

Mr. Stalvey was giggling. "Lily, it's a complete misunderstanding."

"We fell," said Muddy, and just as she said it, she realized her falling on top of him on the sofa, Stalvey grabbing her behind, Muddy's comment, their shifting and his giggling all would be reported to Timothy and Anthony before sundown.

"Maybe I should come back later," Lily said.

"No, not at all," said Muddy. "Mr. Stalvey was just leaving."

He quickly thanked Muddy again for paying for the glass and for the tea, though he hadn't had any and said he would call later to which Muddy just nodded. Once he was out the door, Lily closed it.

"Mother, exactly what is going on here?"

"I'm telling you the truth. Nothing."

"I heard his giggling, your remark about his hands on your behind."

Muddy began to laugh herself. "Lord have mercy," she said. "He came over to thank me, I offered him a glass of tea, then when I was handing it to him, he asked me out, and I spilled it on him. I guess because I was so shocked, we lost our balance and fell to the sofa. It was awkward, but that was it."

"Are you sure, Mama?"

"Of course, I'm sure. I don't have anything to hide."

"Well, are you going to go out with him?"

"Oh, my. I never gave him an answer. I don't know about that."

"Well, I don't see any harm in two elderly people having lunch together."

"Elderly? I'm not 80 yet and I still have some get up and go left it me."

"I didn't mean to offend, and you look good for an older woman in her late seventies."

"Thank you," Muddy said and smiled. "How are the boys?"

"Fine. Why?"

"Just wondering."

"Did they do a good job for you?"

"Yes, of course they did."

"Oh, they love the coats you gave them."

"Your daddy wanted them to have those. You know that."

"I would thank you for the guns, but I'm still upset."

"I know you are, but you should really move on. We've covered this. No use dwelling on something like that. Just put them away for safe keeping. I just didn't think they should be here in case my house gets broken into and they get stolen."

"I understand that, Mama. You know, it made the paper for Christ sakes."

"Don't you use the Lord's name like that. So, the story made the paper?"

"Yeah."

Muddy giggled. "It's been a while since I've made the paper."

"When were you in the paper?"

"Obits. Your daddy's was the last one."

Lily shook her head. "Are you going to Clara's visitation and funeral?"

"Yes."

"I did get flowers from us."

"Good."

"I hate that she killed herself."

"Did they determine that it was a suicide?"

"Yes."

"It is a shame."

"You think she'll go to hell?"

"I don't know. I don't think God smiles favorably upon suicide, but God is loving and forgiving, and we don't know what Clara's life was like. Depression is a disease and they don't know as much as they should. I believe there have been times when we all have it. Some of us come back and some don't. It's a shame, no matter which way you look at it."

"Yes, it is. I know we changed the subject, but the newspaper mentioned Stalvey had been hurt in the incident. What happened to him? He wasn't shot, obviously."

"I should've called you, but I was so frazzled my window was shot out, Stalvey's window was shot out, the police were here and there, they thought he was shot, an ambulance was here, people were driving by, people calling. I just had to lie down and escape it all, but they thought he was shot. The noise startled him and he slipped, bumped his head and passed out. He's fine."

"Well, I'm just thankful you and the boys weren't hurt. I need to get going. I'm on my way to an event in Hahira and thought I'd stop by."

"What kind of event in Hahira?"

"A girl I know from school opened a shop there and she's having a grand opening. I promised I would come. You want to go?"

"No, I'm tired and wanted to rest before the visitation."

"Alright. I'll see you tonight."

"Bye," said Muddy.

Muddy rested for about an hour and a half. She decided she might better eat something before going to Thomasville in case none of her children wanted to eat supper, but she chanced it. She really enjoyed seafood from George and Louie's. Plus, she liked their atmosphere. They'd taken an old hamburger restaurant that had closed and made it into a nice, open and airy, and even elegant little place to eat. She loved their cheese grits and fried green tomatoes. Once she was ready, Muddy made her way out the back door and to the car, leaving the porch light on. The drive to Thomasville wasn't long, and Muddy enjoyed seeing the sites along the way: plantations with pines, ponds, blueberry or vegetable fields. Occasionally she might see a buck and slow the car just in case he decided to jump onto the road in front of her car, and every once in a while, she might have the opportunity to see a flying squirrel or a fox. She hadn't seen a fox in some time. Muddy was early to the funeral home and parked in a handicapped space near the ramp. There were only a handful of cars, but she figured the family would be there and she could sit down before the crowd arrived.

Many of Clara's cousins were there with their children, and Claude's one sister and her husband from Albany, were there. Muddy hugged them all, and she was genuine in telling them how glad she was to see them. In the viewing room, Muddy thought Clara looked about as good as one could in a casket, and she noted they'd fixed her face so she'd be seen as smiling. She thought the lasting smile was good for someone who hadn't smiled that much because of depression. She was struck by several jars with lids sitting around the casket and inquired of the attendant close by: "Oh, yes, those are Ms. Clara's pets."

"Pets?"

"Yes mam, apparently she had had quite a few pets through the years and as they died, she had them cremated, so they could be buried with her. All of them will be placed in the casket with her before we go to the burial tomorrow afternoon."

"I thought she was depressed, but sounds like she was a little crazy, too."

The funeral home attendant smiled and said, "Yes mam," and Muddy walked on to a Queen Anne sofa in the parlor area, where she sat next to Claude's sister Shirley.

"Shame, ain't it?" Shirley said.

"Yes, it is."

"We shouldn't have to bury the younger generation."

"We're lucky we didn't lose any," Muddy said and added, "knock on wood." She tapped the strip of wood in the arm of the sofa.

"Hadn't seen ya'll in a while. You doing well, Shirley?"

"I'm doing alright. My arthritis bothers me more than anything."

"I know. I have some if you ever run out that I'll gladly give you." They both chuckled. "Ya'll have any damage from that tornado?"

"Just a few limbs that's all."

"Did you see that woman and her trailer folded up in that stand of trees on the news over there?"

"No, what happened?"

"Lord, she had a comb stuck in her hair when she was on TV. These younger people don't have any sense about how to look."

"You got that right."

Muddy noted Timothy and his wife coming in, followed by Anthony, and then Lily and Sid, minus the boys. Muddy thought they all looked rather good and certainly looked good in comparison to some of their cousins who weren't as blessed with DNA. Timothy, like a lawyer, was shaking hands and smiling and scanning the room, finding his mama on the sofa and nodded. Muddy nodded back, and in a moment, Timothy was in front of her.

"Hey Mama; hey Aunt Shirley."

"Hey," they both said at the same time.

"Mama, how's Mr. Stalvey?"

"He's fine."

"You need to tell me anything?"

"I don't think so, but you're welcome to take me to dinner at George and Louie's and in return, you'll get all the information you want."

"Mama, that's called blackmail."

"Not when it's your mama." He shook his head and walked off.

"What's he on your case about, Charlotte?"

"Oh, we had a bit of a situation at my house earlier this week. I gave Lily and Sid's boys Claude's guns, and one went off, went through my window and to the old man's window across the street. I really hadn't had time to tell any of them about it, but they found out through others and are a little mad about it. It was fine." Muddy didn't want to get into the incident with her toppling over with Stalvey onto the sofa, him getting fresh, and Lily seeing all this. She didn't think Shirley would care because Claude had been deceased for years, but Muddy just didn't believe in airing all one's business.

"Thank the Lord nobody was hurt," Shirley said.

"Yes."

Later at George and Louie's, Muddy sat with her children, plus Sid and Timothy's wife Nancy, and Timothy was the one who, after their drinks had been delivered, raised the issue.

"You and Mr. Stalvey dating?"

"What?"

"You heard me, Mama," Timothy said.

Muddy cut her eyes at Lily. "We most certainly are not. He came over to thank me for the check I sent him for his window and I offered him some tea. I spilled some and went back to get a wet cloth, and when I got back, he asked me if

I'd like to go eat, and I was taken aback, stumbled without my cane, tossed the tea on him, lost my balance, and fell on top of him on the sofa. I was very embarrassed and humiliated. It is rather humorous now, however, the more I think about it. I guess he was nervous, asking me out."

"Well, we'd be concerned if you become involved with Mr. Stalvey."

"You turning a glass of tea into an affair? Ya'll are as bad as Velma Anderson, but you know what? What does it matter if I go out with him or anyone else? It's none of your business."

"Now, Mama, don't get riled up. I don't want you to have a spell." Everyone paused and smiled, attempting to disguise the tension while the waitress handed out the platters of food.

Muddy picked up her fork once the waitress had gone and pointed it at Timothy. "I'm not riled up. Yet. I'm not going to get remarried or anything, but I might go to dinner with Mr. Stalvey if I want. Beats sitting home all the time by myself. Anthony's about the only one of you who will come take me anywhere. Look, I loved your father, and I would much rather him still be here, but my last days shouldn't be laid up in a nursing home."

"We hope we don't have to put you in one," Lily said.

"I might have something to say about that, too, you know," Muddy said.

"Mama, we just didn't want any older man taking advantage of your money or anything."

"I don't have any major money, but it's your inheritance you are really concerned about here. Well, don't that beat all. I'd hoped I'd raised you all better than that. You'd rather me go on and kill myself like Clara laid out across town in her casket, so you could swoop on over like vultures and have your pick? Your daddy said it was fine."

"Of course, not, Mama. We're just concerned. That's all. What do you mean by Daddy said it was fine."

Nothing was said for a few minutes and Muddy finally said, "Ya'll don't have a thing to worry about, okay? I hear your daddy whispering every once in a while."

Muddy could tell they were looking at each other and thinking she was crazy and she added, "I'm not crazy. I like it. He tells me things."

"Like what?" Lily asked.

"Oh, nothing like 'here are the lottery numbers for the week.' He just calls me back to myself when I'm drifting sometimes or tells me it's okay. It's gentle and soothing, the way he used to touch you all on the shoulder or in the small of your back guiding you, nudging you."

Lily'd teared and Anthony, too. When the waitress walked by, Timothy handed her a card and said he'd get it. He wanted to redirect. "Mama, you want to ride with me and Nancy tomorrow or you want to drive."

"I think I'll drive and let the top down."

"The top?"

"Oh, I'm sorry. I was remembering the Nash your daddy and I had and how I enjoyed the top being off, so the wind could blow my hair. It felt so good and smelled good, too when the Ligustrum were blooming." Muddy hoped heaven smelled like Ligustrum in bloom, but looked like flowers and not a hedge, and she imagined Clara as a spirit meandering through a maze of flowers surrounded by winged angels with hymn music playing softly in the background and seeing her parents and grandparents and Claude and all the generations welcoming her home. Muddy was tired and was ready to get home and get a bath.

"You sure you don't want me to pick you up?"

"Yes, I'm sure, but thanks for the offer."

Chapter 9

In Memory of the victims of September 11, 2001

Clara's funeral had been sad to Muddy because they had a local quartet sing some of Clara's favorite songs: "Precious Memories," "Farther Along," and "Angel Band." Muddy loved these songs, and having them sung barber shop quartet style even added to the beauty of it, yet they depressed Muddy a bit and she wondered if Clara had listened to a lot of this; it might have negatively impacted her depression. Muddy then thought it would be really disturbing if the songs had pushed her to the edge of the suicide cliff, where she took the long fall down.

Muddy liked "Farther Along" better than most because she felt the song was reassuring and we would understand all the tragedy over time. She certainly hoped so, because there had plenty of them through time she didn't understand no matter how hard she tried. 9-11, for example. She wondered what sort of god the extreme Muslims believed in who'd done that. Of course, she wondered that about extreme Christians like those at Waco. One thing Muddy was convinced of and that was none of them believed in the real God most everyone else believed in. All she could do was pray for them, but it seemed like stupid people had been around since the beginning of time. At one time, Muddy thought it might be a good idea if there was something that could take stupid people out of the gene pool, but after thinking about it, she figured we needed stupid people in order to survive. If everyone was smart, then Muddy didn't know how the world would work. She'd even seen a study on 60 Minutes where some researchers had developed a drug that when given to rats reversed the aging process, and she was hopeful, but after thinking about it, she knew it would cause chaos in society if we could cure all these illnesses and extend life. She knew Social Security would collapse. Plus, she wondered why anyone would want to keep on living. In fact, Muddy had a terrible thought that she quickly dismissed from consciousness and thought she would never think it again. She wondered if life could be extended, then there might not even be a need for religion, and this made her question God overall, which gave her a chill and kerplunk at the same time and she shivered in the pew at the church and reached up and gripped the wooden pew in front.

Anthony looked at Muddy and mouthed, "You okay?"

Muddy nodded and removed her hand. She hated to have such thoughts in church and especially at Clara's funeral. She'd always been that way, though, half-listening when church got boring. Muddy made up her mind not to think of such thoughts again, and she wouldn't. She had the ability to close doors in her mind, never to reopen. She considered this a talent because it had taken training from childhood to be able to do it, and she was good at it: she'd dismissed her friend's sexual assault in high school by a coach, she'd dismissed her cousin's robbing a liquor store over in Lakeland, and she'd dismissed Claude's indiscretion of reading nude magazines in the barn. Muddy didn't avoid and dismiss, however. She confronted, did what she could to help or change behavior, and finally dismissed. She knew she'd understand it more one day.

Muddy had spent hours talking with her friend about the sexual assault from the coach, but her friend would not tell. She found the wad of money in her cousin's closet when she was looking for a basket to collect vegetables from their garden and confronted him. She'd read their paper, and she knew he was missing during the time period of the robbery, and she saw the ski mask in his back pocket when he got home. He would not confess, and she did not tell. When she caught Claude looking at the nude pictures in the barn, she had crept in, having had suspicions, and he was surprised, walking up to her, rubbing against her legs. She asked him if he needed something different and he told her no, but they had relations in the barn that day, her looking back and hoping the wire on the door stayed on the nail and remained closed, so the children didn't see.

After the burial, Anthony had asked Muddy if she wanted to ride to Marianna since he'd taken off, and she said yes. They had a quick lunch at the Subway on the Tallahassee road before jumping on I-10 to Marianna. They crossed the Apalachicola River Bridge, and Muddy could tell Anthony was nervous. He didn't like bridges. Both his hands gripped the wheel and he was looking straight ahead.

"You want me to drive?"

"No, Mama, but thanks for offering."

"Why do you think you get so nervous driving?"

"I don't know. I'm not nervous when I know the road, but it's been a while and I forgot about that bridge."

"Well, I think it's okay to be cautious, and you always have been, but when it comes to the point that you freeze up, then maybe you ought to figure out why."

"I know it doesn't do any good to confront the fear, because I just did and I'm still nervous."

"Get you some medicine. That'll take care of it."

"I don't drive far enough to get any medicine."

"That's true. You think we're going to learn anything at the boy's school?"

"I don't know, but I think we'll all feel better knowing something."

"I think you're right."

It was mid-afternoon when they pulled in the sand rut drive that lead to the Florida School for the Boys. The white washed block and wood buildings were clean, there wasn't a great deal of landscaping, and there weren't many cars in the parking lot of the main building, a two-story Georgian-style building with a dedication marker. Muddy didn't want to read it and she felt whoever it was dedicated to wouldn't want it to be given what had gone on there. It didn't give her the evil feeling she felt at the marker ceremony for Cassie Harris, but it was eerie. She could see the white crosses, made with PVC pipe, marking graves. Off in the distance, she could see more grave markers.

As they made their way through the double doors to the first office, there was an old and vacant smell about the place. Anthony opened the door for his mother, and she walked in, cane tapping tile.

"Hey there," said the receptionist, smacking gum and quickly scanning Anthony and his left hand ring finger. "Ya'll here to visit somebody?"

"No, Miss, we're here to find out what happened to my nephew who was sent here as a child. Hank Holloway is his name. We never heard nothing from him." Muddy looked at Anthony who had a puzzled look, and Muddy opened her eyes wide and winked.

"When was he here?"

"Oh, I don't know. Sometime in the 1970s, I believe."

"He'd be gone by now," she said.

"Oh, yes, we know, but we're trying to track him down. There's an inheritance, you see. Of course, if he's passed on, perhaps we could fund something here at the school."

"Lord," the receptionist said. "We ain't had that happen lately. Should I get the administrator, Mr. Dollimer?"

"That won't be necessary. Not yet, anyway. Perhaps we could check some records, so you don't have to, honey? I know you're busy."

"I don't mind. Let me just tell him I'm giving ya'll a tour and then we'll go to where they keep the records."

"Oh, bless your sweet heart," Muddy said. The receptionist sashayed toward a smoke-filled office, opened the door, said something, looked back and smiled, closed the door and returned. "What's your name, honey?"

"That's it."

"Excuse me?" Muddy said.

"Honey, that's my name." She guffawed and Anthony and Muddy forced smiles. "Ya'll just follow me. I ain't been here long. I'm in college and am working here part time. They can't hardly find anybody to work here because of all the bad news through the years."

"We heard about that," Anthony said. "Is it all true?"

"I don't know if it is or not. They told me it's not, but the place is just creepy. I think it's haunted. I won't work out here by myself I'll tell you that. I'll go to McDonald's and flip burgers before I work out here by myself. They're talking about digging up some of the grounds back behind the other building because the number of boys that died don't add up. Who knows? I lived here my whole life and I never heard nothing about it."

"Might be some truth to it all," said Muddy.

Honey shrugged her shoulders and stopped in front of a solid oak door with no window. Once open, Honey said, "Let me show ya'll how this is organized. The years are on the drawers, so all you got to do is go through the 1970s. Usually, they're listed by last name."

"Sounds easy enough," said Anthony.

"I'm supposed to stay with ya'll because some people've tried to steal records, but that's kind of dumb, really."

"Why would it be dumb?" Muddy asked.

"If they did beat, rape, and kill boys, then they wouldn't have put it in the records. They would've hid it all somewhere else, if they recorded it at all."

"That does make sense," Muddy said. "I can tell you're going to be a successful young lady when you get out of college."

"Why thank you. I think so, too. I've tried everything. Even went to beauty school and did nails for a while, but I said to myself, 'Honey, you got a future, and it aint' here.' If I can get me a nursing degree, I'm gonna move to Tallahassee or Tampa, and I'll have a better life than anybody around here. Ain't nothing here for me."

"That's great," Anthony said. "With your personality, I believe you'll make a great nurse." He winked at Muddy.

"Here we go. 1970s. I got a key to open this somewhere. Here. Alright. What did you say your nephew's name was?"

"Hank Holloway," Muddy said.

"How you spell it?"

Anthony spelled it.

"Here. Holloway. Ain't no Hank in here. There's a Henry."

"That's probably it. We called him Hank. His real name was Henry," Muddy said.

"Let's see," said Honey. "Says here this boy was from Morven, Georgia. Is that where ya'll are from?"

"It is," said Muddy.

"Where's that?"

"It's a small community close to Thomasville, which is about thirty miles north of Tallahassee."

"Oh yeah, I think I went there once for a pageant," Honey said. "Ya'll want to look through here. I have no idea what to look for."

"Well, if we could find a discharge record or where his forwarding address is, that might be of some help," Muddy said. She flipped some papers, and commented, "Seems like he was taken to the infirmary a lot. Says here he had a broken leg and arm, had several viruses, too." The very last page she looked at was a form with his information and a note that read, "Run away."

"Lord," Muddy said.

"You find something, Mama?" Anthony was staring at the pictures of the buildings and grounds over time, various directors, visits from dignitaries such as Florida governors and other elected officials.

"The last entry says he ran away."

"Well, that would've been tough to do with all this razor wire they got here, but he might've got out," said Honey. "One man who ran away tried to sue a while back, claimed they shot him as he went under the fence and headed for the swamp, where he near about died, until someone fishing found him and took him to Quincy to a preacher's house and the preacher got him home. Statute of limitations had done run out and he couldn't prove none of it. My boss, Mr. Dollimer told me you can't believe nobody. People hear about the rumors and make up stories to sue for money. That and play the lottery. It's a shame."

"What a story," Anthony said.

"Can we look around the grounds some?" Muddy asked.

"Sure," said Honey. The only building occupied by boys is the last one. You can't get in there unless somebody opens the door, but I would tell you to stay away from them. Some of them are mean and disgusting. You won't believe what they do. Just the sight of them dirty and sweaty bothers me."

"Well, honey, you have been so sweet to help us, stay with us, and we appreciate it. I guess we know Hank didn't die here and maybe we'll be able to find him. We'll just have to keep looking."

"I sure do hope ya'll find him," she said.

"We do, too. Do you have a card, Honey, so we can contact you or Mr. Dollimer and keep you updated, in case he's passed on and some of the inheritance could come here?"

"Sure do. Got a whole stack of them. Mr. Dollimer keeps trying to give them out to people. He's gonna move up in government. You watch. The man will be in Tallahassee in the capital before you know it."

"I'm sure he will," said Anthony, turning and smiling at his mother who returned the smile.

"Here you go," Honey said, pulling one from her jacket pocket.

"Thanks," said Anthony. "It was good to meet you."

"Same here."

Honey turned to lock the door, and Muddy and Anthony made their way down the hall and out the door. They walked down the sidewalk, made their way to a small white concrete block building. A plaque read "Infirmary." Muddy sat on a metal bench nestled between the sidewalk and driveway. Anthony stood shifting from one foot to another.

"You want to walk to the graveyard, Mama?"

"I'm getting kind of tired," Muddy said. "I need to rest for a bit. You go on."

"I'm not interested in seeing them," he said. "Plus, we know Hank ain't out there."

"No, we know he's not in one of the marked graves. He could be in one of the unmarked ones."

"True," Anthony said. "By the way, you were pretty good back there. You could get an academy award. How'd you come up with that?"

"I was thinking on the way down here what I might say to get a peek at his records, and I figured he might be a long lost nephew or something. I don't know. Really, I had a bunch of different ideas swirling around in my mind, and then it just kind of came out. I know it was a lie, but the Lord is for forgiving and I don't believe he much cares if it's for the good."

Anthony laughed. "I'm gonna walk over here and see if this building's open." Muddy sat there fanning gnats with an old church bulletin she pulled out of her purse.

"Lord, it's humid," she said to herself. She closed her eyes and she could see Hank Holloway waiving at her from her yard while he played baseball with Anthony, Timothy, and Lily. Muddy waived back from the swing and told them not to chase a ball in the road without looking both ways first. As Muddy watched them more, she focused on Hank Holloway and it seemed Muddy had a zoom lens and could see him up close. She heard a whisper: "Go in." Muddy was startled and opened her eyes. She grabbed the cane, pulled herself up, and walked toward the infirmary. It was clean, but there was graffiti on the walls and stains.

"Mama, I thought you were tired. Ain't nothing in here to see. They have some displays of old nursing equipment and photos of boys, all happy looking."

"If I were under investigation, I'd do that, too, and I would leave the graffiti to show they didn't punish them for everything."

Muddy walked around the room, read some of the graffiti. Some of it read "Ziggy was here," some it said someone loves someone else, one read somebody's mama wore combat boots, and as Muddy turned, she noted one was written in what she thought was a foreign language, but once she got close up to it, she called Anthony. "Look at this."

"Jibberish," he said.

"No, it's not." She pulled a compact mirror from her purse held it up, stood by the wall and read it. "It's signed Hank Holloway. He did run away. Says he's going on top of old Smokey."

"I'll be damned."

"Well, maybe he did run away to the Smokey mountains. I hope he made it. Least he tried. We'll have to get Timothy to check the computer."

"The internet, Mama."

"You know what I mean. Call him on your cell phone." Anthony did call him, left him a message that they were in Marianna, getting ready to head home, and let him know what they'd discovered. He directed Timothy to do searches in the Tennessee/North Carolina region to see if he could locate him. He told him it was probably a long shot that he would have run away there, stayed there all these years.

"Let's go," Muddy said, as they made their way to Anthony's car.

On the ride home, Muddy rested. She told Anthony if it made him feel better to take the back roads up to Bainbridge, then to Thomasville, and then on to Morven, which he did, adding the scenery would be better, but Muddy knew there wasn't much to see, not now and not nearly two hundred years ago when the European people started settling the area. They stopped for supper in Thomasville and ate at the Plaza, which had a buffet of catfish and chicken with an array of vegetables. The building and décor were dated, but the service and food were consistently good. Muddy particularly liked their banana pudding, but felt the serving wasn't large enough. Of course, she didn't need much, so it was alright and she didn't say anything.

"Mama, I'll drop you by the funeral home to get your car. You alright to drive home?"

"Of course I am," she said.

Muddy made the drive home from Thomasville, just like she had through the years, and she pulled under the carport, grabbed her cane, and made her way into the house. She plopped her purse on the counter and poured herself a glass of iced tea, sat in her lift chair, kicked off her pumps, and watched the news. She was definitely tired, but it was too early for her warm milk and too early to go to sleep. She didn't want to wake up at three in the morning and not be able to get back to sleep, so she decided to stay up. She'd watched the news for about thirty minutes before she saw the red light blinking on her answering machine. She pushed play, and the first message was from Fred Stalvey who told her again how sorry he was for the fall and the misunderstanding and how he hoped the service for Clara was a nice one. Muddy thought it was a nice message. Next was a sales call from India, and Muddy didn't know what he was saying any more than the man at the Suwannee Swifty and figured when she answered and got that call again, she'd refer him to the Suwannee Swifty. Lily told her they were Hindus, but Muddy didn't know anything about what that meant. She figured they were Muslim and suspected they might be terrorists come to blow up people in small towns. Muddy knew if they wanted to get attention, that attacking the twin towers or Washington DC or just flying a plane into the ground certainly got it. America was forever changed and Muddy had a shoebox full of just 9-11 articles. She knew the angels had helped those victims cross, and she shuttered at what she believed God was going to do to terrorists. She thought that if Muslim terrorists wanted to take on America, they'd need to take out the bridges or the railroad and maybe even invade rural America, and it was just like them to get into all the Suwannee Swiftys to do it.

The next message was from Timothy who said, "Mama, I know you ain't going to believe this, but I think I might have found Hank Holloway in the Tennessee mountains. Give me a call when you get home."

Muddy felt excited. She imagined it to be what the Pentecostals must feel on Sunday mornings when they get the spirit. Their church was just down the road a bit, and when they got to rocking, she could hear them from her porch. She'd never been, but she heard stories of miraculous healings, speaking in tongues, and wild dancing. She dialed his number.

"Hey, Timothy. What in the world have you found out?"

"I found a Hank Holloway living in Sevierville, Tennessee. He's a preacher. I called and left a message on his answering machine, but he didn't call the office back before I had to leave for a Chamber meeting."

"You reckon that's him?"

"I don't know. I certainly hope so."

"Me, too."

"Well, let me know what you hear."

"I will. Have a good night."

Muddy was happy and felt good about Timothy taking the initiative to check further and then to make a call. She soaked in the tub a while, surrounded herself with suds, and almost fell asleep. "It's okay," Claude whispered. "What's okay?" she said aloud. When she dried herself, she put on her gown and headed to the kitchen to warm her milk, and read before finally falling asleep. About ten o'clock, the phone rang, and Muddy slurred, "Hello."

"Hey, did I wake you?" Timothy asked.

"That's alright," Muddy said.

"I found him. He just called, and it's the same Hank Holloway."

"Thank the Lord. Tell me about it."

"Well, he was a bit stand-offish at first, but when I told him who I was, where I was from, and so on, he jumped right in and we talked for about thirty minutes."

"That's great." Muddy felt a peace come over she hadn't felt in a couple of weeks. To her, it felt like a phlebotomist had loosened the tourniquet on her arm after drawing blood.

"Here's the real good news. They're going to Disney tomorrow and are going to stop and spend the night in a motel at the Hahira exit off I-75. I told them if they'd like to eat supper, we could go to the Catfish house in Hahira. My treat. He agreed, so if you can get Anthony and Lily, and ya'll come to Hahira tomorrow at six o'clock, we'll have a Hank Holloway reunion."

"That's great, Timothy. I'll call them first thing in the morning. I'm so excited. I hope I can get back to sleep."

"See you tomorrow." They hung up, and Muddy turned on the light and went to the kitchen to get some more warm milk. She heard a rustling outside the living room window. The sheers were closed, but the drapes were tied back. She figured a branch from the azaleas must be scratching on the glass, but she turned on the porch light and opened the front door. The screen was latched.

"Someone there?"

"Muddy," she heard a whisper. "You up?"

"Who is that?"

"Fred."

"Fred, why are you whispering and what are you doing in the bushes peeking in my window? Have you lost your mind?"

"No, I walked over here and was checking to see if you were awake before I knocked."

"I was asleep, but Timothy called and woke me up. Come on in. I've got some good news to share with you."

"What is it?"

"We've found Hank Holloway. He's a preacher in the mountains of Tennessee."

"That's great!"

"I know. I feel so good about it. Anthony and I went to the Florida School for Boys after Clara's funeral in Thomasville. We found his records and it noted run-away. I figured they'd shot him or something, but thank the Lord, he was a run-away. We called Timothy on the way back from Marianna, and he checked the computer, found him, and left him a message. Here's the best part. They are coming through on their way to Disney World tomorrow and we're going to meet them at the catfish house in Hahira. You've got to go with us!"

"So, are you asking me out?"

Muddy laughed. "I guess I am."

"Sure, I'll go."

"What did you come over here for anyway?"

"I was coming over to see if you were still mad. I left you a message and you didn't call back."

"Well, I wasn't here and was too tired."

"Are you still mad, then?"

"No," Muddy said. "I'm not mad one bit."

"So, can we go out some time without the family and Hank Holloway's family?"

Muddy laughed. "Sure, but you better get out of here because Velma Anderson's probably driving around Morven trying to stir up a story."

"Good night, Charlotte" Fred said.

"Good night." Muddy locked the door, but waited until Stalvey had made it across the street before she turned the porch light off. She walked back to her bedroom, got under the quilt, and rubbed her feet together. Part of Muddy had wanted Stalvey to stay a while.

Chapter 10

For the 1.3 million women abused in the U.S. each year

The next day leading up to the Holloway get together came quickly. Muddy awoke early to the birds chirping. She felt peaceful and had slept well, but there was still a lot that bothered her about visiting the Florida School for the Boys: how many investigations needed to be done before someone actually took action, how many people in the world turned their heads, either rationalizing or completely ignoring problems, how many victims and survivors didn't have happy endings like Hank Holloway, how many people could deny evil exists in this world when so much evil is done? There were so many questions that she couldn't answer, and she didn't think most people could answer them either. She felt like if only more people became involved, if more people put their religious beliefs behind them on a daily basis to fight back, especially those who weren't impacted directly, then more would be done. Muddy knew that we were all part of the human race and all of the evil impacted all of us, both spiritually and financially.

When she got up, she was hungry and cooked eggs, bacon, and toast. She sat in her lift chair and ate her breakfast while watching the news. She wondered about Clara and her depression and figured if she watched the news, it wouldn't have helped any: more killed by al Qaeda, the spread of SARS and the death toll rising, the fallout from Catholic priests scandals, and of course losing Bob Hope and Katherine Hepburn. To know they would no longer be entertaining people was enough to depress anyone. With one click of the remote, all of the far away bad news faded from sight, and Muddy readied herself for the day.

Muddy's intention was to clip some flowers, to clean the kitchen, and to wash her bed linens, but before this, she needed to call Anthony and Lily about the reunion at the Catfish House. Anthony was very excited, but he seemed disappointed that Hank had made a preacher. Lily, on the other hand, was excited. She told Muddy she didn't know if Sid and the boys would come or not, but she would try. Muddy told both Anthony and Lily she would drive herself. Her work busied her until lunch, and she'd planned on a light lunch and a small nap in the afternoon before getting ready for the dinner at the Catfish House in Hahira.

Muddy tapped down the hall to get her bed linens she'd stripped from her bed and got the washer going. When they finished washing, she would've preferred they dry in the sun, but the South Georgia sky was overcast due to the spread of clouds from a tropical depression in the Gulf, and she decided it might be best to toss them in the dryer. She cleaned the sink and counters in the kitchen and swept, though there was little trash on the floor given she was the only one living in the house now. She mopped with Pine-Sol and breathed the scent deeply, imagining herself just outside Morven in the pine forests that surrounded the town. Fortunately, even when the timber companies logged the trees, most land owners replanted, knowing it might take thirty years or so before they turned a profit on their labor. Outside, Muddy used her pruning shears to cut enough roses to have on the kitchen table. She thought of Fred Stalvey, but told herself, "You are not cutting these to impress Fred Stalvey. You are cutting these for you to enjoy." Sometimes, Muddy thought she was going to just go crazy, hearing whispers she believed to be Claude, talking to herself, and thinking too much, but she reassured herself she had always been this way, even in childhood. She knew that as people aged, they thought they were getting worse when, in fact, they'd always been the same way, but wanted something to blame it on, which would be age.

Tasks completed, Muddy had a light lunch of ham and leftover peas from the fridge she warmed in the microwave. It was enough to sustain her, and while she probably didn't need the salt, she wouldn't swell from it, like most of her Sunday School class. After about an hour nap, Muddy got up and watched reruns of the Andy Griffith show. She liked him, imagined herself to be level-headed like him. She liked Aunt Bee, too, but she was mostly annoyed with Barney. She felt like he was an extreme character, and while she thought most police in small towns were probably like Barney because they were trained for action, but never had any, they stored up this energy they had to release. She thought Aunt Bee's friend Clara was a little like Velma Anderson, though they didn't look the same. Some of her favorite episodes were when the Darling's sang with Andy. She thought they should've been featured even more, and though she thought he was crazy, she liked Ernest T. Bass and figured other than Crazy Jenny, there was probably someone around Morven like Ernest T. It was getting late in the afternoon, and Muddy decided she'd do something different. She picked up her phone and dialed Fred's number. It was memorized, not because she called Fred Stalvey often, but when Charlene was alive, Muddy called her often.

"Hello?"

"Fred, did you still want to ride over to Hahira and eat supper with us and the Hank Holloway family at the Catfish House?"

"Sure. What time do you want to leave?"

"Well, I think we're supposed to be there at 6:00, so we should probably leave about a quarter till, don't you think?"

"Yeah, then we'll be there just a little early or right on time. You want me to drive, Charlotte?"

"That's fine."

"You mind riding in the Thunderbird with the top down?"

"There're some clouds. You think it might rain?"

"No, I don't think so, but I'll put the top up if it does."

"That's fine with me." Muddy made a note to look for a nice scarf just in case and remembered the Nash and how much she enjoyed riding with the top down.

"I'll pull around back and pick you up," said Stalvey.

"I can walk over there," Muddy said.

"No, it's fine. I'll just pick you up."

"Alright." On the one hand, Muddy thought it was silly that two 70-something year olds were bogged down in such a discussion, particularly given the fact they only lived across the street from each other, and Muddy knew the minute she stepped into the Thunderbird that she was doomed to become the whore of Morven in the eyes of Velma Anderson and the other gossips who, secretly, were after Fred Stalvey themselves. She laughed out loud as she headed down the hall to get ready. The irony to Muddy was that she wasn't after Fred Stalvey. They'd been friends many years ago and were simply spending time together. Muddy thought about being queen for a day. She'd make Velma and all the other lazy, no count people line up one by one and she'd give them each a task to complete: help the homeless, help the abused, help the alcoholics and drug addicts, and so on. This would keep them focused on something useful and out of her business and everyone else's business.

Muddy dressed in linen slacks, a nice blouse that matched a scarf and purse she had, and sandals. She'd given herself a manicure and pedicure before Clara's visitation, so she felt pretty good and confident in how she looked. When the doorbell rang, she turned on the front porch light, then went to the back door and turned that porch light on. She opened the door and went out to meet Fred Stalvey who was at the bottom of the steps, sporting khakis, polo, and loafers. He'd lost a lot of hair, but what he had left seemed groomed. The top was down on the powder blue T-bird, and Fred held the door for Muddy and she stepped in, putting her cane to the side.

As they pulled out of Muddy's drive, and onto Highway 122, they cruised through town heading East to Hahira, and several people gawked. Of course Muddy had on her sunglasses, as did Fred Stalvey, but people knew who they were. The wind felt good to Muddy, but she had a hard time hearing what Stalvey was saying because of the wind and because her left ear was covered by the scarf.

"I've thought about putting my house on the market," Stalvey said.

"What?"

He repeated himself, and Muddy said, "Farmer's market wasn't open today."

Fred Stalvey shook his head, and Muddy turned to look at him. "I'm talking about selling my house."

She understood him. "Why?"

"Market's high. I thought about buying one of those small condos in town. It's all on one floor. Less upkeep for me."

"I thought you had someone come in and clean."

"I mean the maintenance of it all. Owning an older home has a lot of upkeep."

"That's true," Muddy said. "Might not be a bad idea."

They didn't say much as the T-bird accelerated to fifty-five, and Muddy enjoyed the sites. They passed over the river bridge and Muddy thought about Cassie Harris, and they passed the peach shed outside Barney. Muddy loved the look of the peach orchards and thought it might be nice to have a house surrounded by orchards, but someone told her there would be a lot of bugs, particularly bees, because of the fruit. As they neared Hahira, they crossed over the interstate and headed just inside the city limits, where the Catfish House was located, in a stand of pecan trees next to the Harvey's grocery store. She noticed Anthony's car, and he was sitting in a rocking chair on the porch. When the T-bird pulled into the parking space, Muddy waived and Anthony stood.

"Hey," she said.

"Mama?"

"Hey Anthony," said Stalvey.

Anthony nodded and said hello, but it wasn't loud.

"What a ride," Muddy said as she propped her cane on the pavement and climbed out, Stalvey holding the door. He laughed.

"I thought you wanted to drive," said Anthony. "I would've picked you up."

"No, I wanted to ride with Mr. Stalvey in his convertible. I hadn't been in a convertible for years. Anybody else here yet?"

"I don't think so," said Anthony, and about that time, the Catfish House door opened, and a man said, "Mrs. Rewis?"

"Yes?"

"I thought that was you. I'm Hank Holloway."

"Muddy opened her arms and they embraced. You remember Anthony?"

Hank and Anthony shook hands, and Stalvey introduced himself, again, as well. "Well, I'll be. I'd a never recognized you after all this time," he said.

"I don't think I'd a recognized you either," Anthony said.

"Ya'll come on in. Timmy must've reserved a whole room in the back for us. I want ya'll to meet my family."

"Have ya'll heard the news today?" asked Hank.

"What's happened," asked Stalvey.

"They got Saddam Hussein. I heard it on the radio about an hour ago."

"That's great," said Muddy. "I was beginning to wonder if they'd ever get him."

"He's gonna have to stand trial for crimes against humanity," said Hank.

"Shouldn't even have a trial," said Stalvey.

"Now, Mr. Stalvey," said Anthony. "Everyone has to be tried first."

"I know," Stalvey said "But sometimes I just don't think some deserve it."

They all nodded as they went inside and made their way to the backroom. Hank introduced them to his wife, a stout lady with a wide smile, a teenage daughter and son, both seemingly reserved. The waitress took drink orders while they made some small talk until Lily, Sid, and Tom came in, followed by Todd and Shaneka. Within minutes, Timothy and Nancy showed as well, and everyone made introductions. Muddy could sense Hank was uncomfortable with Shaneka being there with Todd, and she wondered why.

After the rest had their drink orders taken, Muddy said, "I have something I want to show you." She pulled his letter from her purse. "I found this a couple of weeks ago and didn't recall reading it when it came all those years ago. As everyone will tell you, I was determined to find out what had happened to you and felt so bad about it. Whether you know it or not, Fred and his late wife Charlene tried to adopt you once you were at the Florida School for the Boys. Anyway, we went there, trying to find out something. Me and Anthony even read a message you wrote in reverse on the infirmary wall."

Hank wiped tears from his eyes and said, "I'd forgotten about the writing on the wall. I'd left that for my friends. I don't know if they ever read it or not. Never heard from none of them boys again. The Lord has once again blessed me. I didn't know ya'll tried to adopt me. But I'm glad ya'll contacted me. It means a lot to me and I always thought of ya'll as my family."

Lily and Muddy were wiping tears, but managed to order when the waitress took orders, and Muddy said, "Do you mind telling us about the Boys School and how you got away. I just knew you'd been shot and in one of them unmarked graves."

"Sadly, there are probably several unmarked graves, and the reason I know is that is because that's when they did something nice for all the boys, like taking us to the pool or loading us on the bus for ice cream in town or taking us to church. I'd been in the infirmary for a virus and all the boys were going to town on the bus and I had to stay behind. As soon as the bus pulled off, I saw them digging two graves and carrying boys wrapped in dirty, bloody sheets and dumping them in holes and covering them up. It made me sick. I'd heard about it and knew one of them. Every time I had a chance to go to church, I did. The preacher knew about some of the goings-on and some of the administration that went to church there decided he needed to move on to another church. He told the church on his last night, he had a job in the Smokey mountains, and that's when I said, if I could get away, I'd run up there. I sure didn't know where my Mama was. One night, I woke up and felt like I should walk outside. I did, praying silently to myself, and there was a ball of light that went right into my chest. I don't know what it was, but I knew it was from God. The next night, I felt the strength inside me to go, and I slipped away and ran as far as I could. When the sun come up, I was still running up the highway. I made it up to Cairo, Georgia and caught a ride to Columbus. When I got to a truck stop by I-85, I saw an 18-wheeler with a Tennessee tag and told him I was hitching my way to East Tennessee. He was on his way to Knoxville and bought me some food and let me ride with him. It took me a couple of days to find the preacher, but he came for me and let me stay with them. The Grahams were good to me. They're in a nursing home now and I go by there every day on my way home. When I first got there, they wrote to my Mama, and she gave me permission to stay with them. I figured she was worried her husband might kill me, so she let me stay. They would take me to visit her one day a year, and once in a while, she'd send me a card with some money it. I got back in school, graduated and went to work as a mechanic. I'd learned it in high school. Still do it, but I got folks who do it for me now, while I mainly do the business end and preach on Wednesday night and Sunday."

"Do you know whatever happened to your Mama?" Lily asked.

"Oh yeah, she came to live with us in her final years. The man she married after my daddy died beat her for years, especially when he was drunk, and even when he was dying with cancer. I went down there when he was dying and tried to talk to him, but he was struggling bad. I'm telling you the devil was in this man like I'd never seen, and even at the end, he was seeing all kinds of demons. Mama, she took it and took it through the years. She'd leave him and go to her sister's house in Ocala, but she'd come back to him because he'd say he was sorry and cry and tell her he needed help and needed her. She loved him. I'll give her credit for that. She waited tables and somehow managed to feed them and house them for years in a little trailer until he died. I told her to come stay with us, that she'd suffered enough. And she did. She lived with us about fifteen years. She got into our church, helped Earline keep the house and help with the children and even got involved in the lady's group at church and sang in the choir. I felt so proud; she'd come such a long way. She'd begun to get more sickly, and we found out she had cancer, and by the time we found it, it was too late. She was eat up with it."

"It's an amazing story," said Muddy.

"Sure is," Timothy said and everyone nodded, while the waitress placed the platters around the table, and everyone began to eat.

The conversation became more light, and it turned more toward the children: what clubs and activities they were interested in. Both Hank's teenage children talked and then it switched to Lily and Sid's, and finally, Todd's friend Shaneka.

"Ya'll dating?" Hank asked Todd and Shaneka.

"We're friends," Todd said and Shaneka giggled.

Then, as if slipping from one end of a zip line to another end, Hank said, "Well, that's probably best. I'm not sure the Lord approves of all this interracial relationship stuff." Hank's daughter took her napkin and dabbed the corners of her eyes, and Muddy knew why the girl was being reserved and probably understood the reason for a Disney trip. She decided she would act. If she didn't, no one else would, and she'd be no better off than all those she imagined she'd line up if she were queen for the day.

"I don't know about that," Muddy said.

"How's that, Mrs. Rewis?" Hank asked.

"Well, we had a lesson in Sunday School some time back. I believe it was from Exodus. Moses' sister had criticized him. The lesson indicated it was because she was a prophetess and wanted more attention."

"That's right," Hank said.

But Muddy continued, "She was also being critical of Moses' wife and their relationship because Moses had married a black woman from Ethiopia, which obviously the Lord had blessed. For her criticism, she was turned white

167

by the Lord. She was banished from the camp, but in the end, they prayed for her and she was returned and regained her color. I believe this means God was telling us not to be judgmental of what he has blessed, even if it is interracial relationships."

There was silence at the table, but Muddy noted Hank's daughter smiling. Shaneka and Todd, too. Hank's wife seemed shocked and no one at the table said a word. Muddy added, "Ya'll act like my Sunday School class when I said it. I figured they'd kick me out for that."

"No," said Hank. "The Lord's words can be read in different ways. I've never thought about it like that, and I'll have to go back and check some references about this, but you may be right."

"I don't know if I am or not, but I do think we should all be less judgmental."

Everyone nodded. Timothy took the bill when the waitress brought it and gave her a credit card. As they all stood to leave, Lily asked if Muddy needed a ride home, and Muddy said, "No, I rode in Mr. Stalvey's T-bird." Lily smiled and looked at Timothy who just shrugged. As they stood around a bit more outside, Sid offered Hank some advice about Disney World. Anthony and Timothy talked with Mr. Stalvey, checking his Thunderbird, while Lily, Hank's wife, and Nancy stood with Muddy making small talk about how good the food was and how some of it differed from what they ate in Tennessee.

Hank said to Muddy, "I appreciate you all finding me and caring after all these years. It means a lot to me, and as a preacher I often find myself doubting if people care or not, and just when I do, the Lord blesses me with an experience that proves it. And the good Lord has spoken to me through you on some other issues that I need more time on."

"You were a blessing to us back then, and I hope to our future as well," Muddy responded, as Stalvey helped her to the T-bird, where she sat, tying on her scarf for the short ride back to Morven. Anthony and Timothy leaned in and said, "Now, Mr. Stalvey, don't be driving like a teenager now, you hear?"

"Ah, you boys. Two old people like us, what kind of trouble could we possibly get into?"

"Speak for yourself, Mr. Stalvey. I'm not old!" Muddy said.

Chapter 11

For those who heal bodies and souls

Muddy and Fred Stalvey were driving back to Morven, and the sun was setting in the distance. There was coolness in the evening spring air, and to Muddy, it felt nice. Combine that with all of the good news at dinner, and Muddy couldn't have felt better. When they got to Barney, they turned left by the peach shed, and Stalvey said, "It's beautiful this evening."

"Yes, it is," Muddy said. "I'm so glad I got to hear Hank Holloway's story."

"It's certainly a good one," Stalvey said.

"Did you really remember him?"

"No," Stalvey said. "Not really. I vaguely recall meeting him at the school and us talking about adoption later after Claude showed us the letter. That's about it. It just never worked out. I think Charlene talked to his mother once."

"It all worked out, though."

"Yes it did," Stalvey said, and the Thunderbird picked up speed, meandering its way through the pine forests of Southern Georgia. As they came into Morven, they passed the Methodist church, and Muddy thought about Claude, not so much about his grave and the corpse in the casket, but about him in his new form in heaven, and she imagined him just across the river waiting for her, standing and hugging her when she crossed. It was a positive image to her. She imagined going for her doctor's checkup in a couple of days and she imagined bad news they might deliver: "Ms. Rewis, we are going to have to do by-pass surgery," or "We've discovered a mass that pressing on your arteries and this is causing you to have the kerplunk sensation and we'll give you six months," or "We think the hardening of the arteries is not allowing you to get enough oxygen." She didn't want to hear any bad news. She had hoped just to close her eyes, fall asleep, and cross to Claude. She didn't want to suffer. Her eyes were closed, her head was tilted back in the Thunderbird on the headrest, and the wind stroked her face, as the antique car roared on. "It's alright," whispered Claude. "What?" Muddy said to herself. "It," said the whisper. Muddy wasn't ready for it.

"You fall asleep, Charlotte?"

"No, just resting my eyes. Past few days have about worn me out."

"You want to get an ice cream and ride around a bit. I'm enjoying this."

"Me, too, but I'm tired. Besides, I don't want an ice cream from the Suwannee Swifty. I don't like going in there."

Stalvey chuckled. "Why not?"

"Stinks."

"Never noticed."

"I would appreciate it if you would just drop me off."

"Don't forget there's Bingo in Dixie tomorrow night."

"I haven't. I do have a check-up in Thomasville the day after, so I don't need to be out late tomorrow night."

"Everything alright?"

"I think so. Routine visit."

"Thomasville?"

"Yes."

"You want me to go with you, drive you?"

"No, I plan to stop by Anthony's, do a little shopping while there. I appreciate it, though. You need me to pick up anything for you while I'm there?"

"No, but I appreciate it. Thanks for inviting me tonight. It meant a lot." The Thunderbird pulled into the gravel drive behind Muddy's house, and Stalvey jumped out, sprinted to her door, and opened it, helping her out. Muddy thanked him again and headed inside.

Muddy walked into the back door, and Fred backed out of her driveway. When she got inside, she peeked out the curtain in the living room to watch Fred pull in his garage, and it closed behind him. She saw lights come on, she sat down in the lift chair, and she turned on the headline news. Part of her felt silly about all of a sudden seeing about him when she had never given him a second thought before.

The Bingo and dance were nice the next evening, except for seeing Velma and knowing their date would be all over town. Muddy didn't care. She had a good time. The next day, Muddy was still tired, not because they had stayed out too late. In fact, Fred had brought her home by 9:00 p.m. She had tossed and turned a lot, thinking about Fred, their slow dance and how it made her feel.

Muddy's doctor's appointment was at 11:30 a.m. in Thomasville. They'd told her not to eat, so she had her morning coffee and a little breakfast bar. She didn't consider that eating and she'd done it this way for years and the blood work was always the same. She liked either an 8:00 a.m. appointment, because she would be first and they wouldn't make her wait that long, except the doctor wasn't always there at 8:00 due to hospital rounds and she didn't like sitting on that plastic pad with paper. She normally took a book to read and sat in the chair, but the chairs weren't comfortable either. She liked the 11:30 a.m. appointment better, though, because she knew they would all go to lunch at noon like clockwork. She felt like they even rushed through some visits just to go eat lunch. She'd witnessed it many times through the years, and while she never revealed her secret to anyone about appointment times and getting seen quicker, she felt like there were others there who knew as well.

When she got to Thomasville at 8:30 a.m., she decided to swing by Anthony's house to say hello and to see if he would like to go to lunch later in the day. She knew it was his day off. When Muddy rang the bell, she could hear some scrambling, and a woman wearing a bathrobe opened the door.

"Yes?"

"Is Anthony here?" For a moment, Muddy thought she may have gone to the wrong house, but looked about, noticed Anthony's car, his Georgia bulldog mailbox, his hedges all neatly trimmed.

"He's taking a shower. Is there something I can help you with?"

"I'm Charlotte Rewis, his mother."

"Oh. Oh my. Let me get him."

"May I come in and sit? Propping on my cane isn't very comfortable."

"Oh, I'm sorry, Mrs. Rewis. Of course you can." She opened the door and held it for Muddy. Muddy mused Lily would really enjoy this scene even more than the scene she found her and Fred Stalvey in the other day. Muddy couldn't wait to see the look on Anthony's face when he came out of the shower. She just hoped he put something on before making an entrance. The comedy of it all was almost too much and she continued to giggle, not so much from an unknown woman in a bathrobe answering Anthony's door, but because it had been a woman. She kept saying to herself, "Thank the Lord; thank the Lord." She even imagined announcing in her Sunday School class that she'd caught Anthony having an affair in Thomasville and to tell them to pray for him just to get their reaction. Anthony was so secretive about his personal life that Muddy had convinced herself that Anthony was probably gay, not that she would have minded so much. She just wanted all her children to live happy and fulfilling lives as she had.

She could hear whispers in the back, and she heard Anthony's voice raise and say, "What?" followed by a "Shhh," and in a moment, Anthony came from the back wearing short pants, a t-shirt, his hair combed, but wet.

"Mama, you should have let me know you were coming and I would have been dressed."

"You are dressed, and you're right that I should have called. It was a spur of the moment thought that I would just stop by on my way to run errands, before my doctor's appointment, and see if you wanted to eat lunch. I called Lily before I left, but I didn't remember you were off until I was on my way, and you know I don't have one of those cell phones."

"So you met Kathy?"

"Well, not formally," Muddy said and Kathy walked toward her and extended her hand to which Muddy replied, "Nice to meet you."

"Good to finally meet you as well."

"Do you work at the Piggly Wiggly?"

"Goodness, no. I work at the college."

"How did you two meet?"

"We met in class."

"Class?"

"Mama, I didn't tell you, but I've been taking classes to get my degree. Should have done it a long time ago, but it's been fun."

"Well, I don't know when I've been happier to hear such good news. I'm proud of you."

"Thanks," he said. "Well, what do you think of Kathy?"

"I think she's fine," Muddy said, smiling. "I guess I should get out of the way and let you two get ready."

"No, you're fine," said Kathy. "Can I get you a cup of coffee?"

"Sure," Muddy said. Kathy walked toward the kitchen.

"I'm a bit embarrassed," Anthony said.

"Nothing to be embarrassed about, Anthony. You're a grown man."

"I know, but still, it's awkward."

"I think it's great. I've often worried about you being alone."

"I guess you'll have to worry about someone else now, like Fred Stalvey."

"No, we're just friends. No one could replace your Daddy."

"I know."

Kathy returned with the coffee and Muddy took a sip.

"That's strong."

"It's Starbucks," she said. "It packs a punch in the morning, and it costs more, but I love it."

"I do, too. Maybe I could get some while I'm here. You sell this at the Piggly Wiggly, Anthony?"

"Yes, we have it there."

"I may need to stop and get some." Muddy sipped the last of the coffee and sat talking to Anthony about Hank Holloway and what a relief it all was to her now while Kathy had slipped into the back and put on clothes. When Kathy returned, Muddy could tell she was a cute lady, well-maintained through the years like Stalvey's Thunderbird, except not quite that old. "I need to get going, if I'm going to run my errands before my appointment," and she stopped, propped on her cane, and said, "We'll be at the Bistro a little after 12 if you want to join us. Kathy, you're welcome to join us as well."

"Thank you, but I have an appointment at lunch. I appreciate the offer. Another time, perhaps."

"Yes," Muddy said, and she noted Kathy's use of perhaps and liked it, not because it indicated a "maybe not," but because it wasn't a word one would use if she was trash. She didn't look like trash and she didn't talk like trash. For Muddy, that was a good indicator she wasn't and confirmation she had raised Anthony right.

Muddy ran her errands in town and then made it to the doctor's office about five minutes early. They handed her a form she had to update even though there were no updates, and she was called back quickly. Weight taken, blood pressure taken, blood drawn and urine specimen collected, Muddy sat in the patient room reading a book. She was just beginning to settle into it on the first page, when the door was flung open and the doctor was there, saying how good everything looked. He was impressed and they would let her know about the blood work in a couple of days. He told her it had been five years since her colonoscopy and she told him that it could wait another five as far as she was concerned. He asked her if she had been having any problems, and she told him about the kerplunks.

"Let me help you onto the table." He pulled out the extension and asked Muddy to lay down. He opened the door, asked for one of the nurses to get something Muddy couldn't quite make out, and the nurse returned with pads, chords. The nurse unbuttoned Muddy's blouse and told her they were going to take an electro cardiogram just to get a baseline heart pattern and the doctor told her he might want to do a stress test. Muddy figured as much and a stress test would lead to something else and medicine or surgery and the doctor would get richer, Muddy poorer, the state and federal governments poorer, and rates would go up even more.

"I doubt I need all that," Muddy said. "It's just every once in a while. In fact, it just did it."

The doctor read the EKG on a computer at the desk, which was next to a glass jar containing cotton balls and tongue depressors. "I see. This is not a big deal. Usually, this is caused by stress, caffeine, things like that."

"Well, I'm under stress right now, and I've had some Starbucks for the first time and I'm feeling kind of jumpy."

He laughed and told the nurse they had what the needed, and she began to remove the pads, which, to Muddy, felt like Band-Aids being ripped from her skin. "Mrs. Rewis, I'm going to write you a little prescription. This is something that will be in generic form, and it's just a small pill that will keep your heartbeat level and you shouldn't feel any side effects from it. Of course, if you lay off caffeine, that might help some, too."

"I'd rather take the pill," she said. "Giving up coffee now might kill me more than the kerplunks."

The doctor handed her the prescription, said he'd see her in a year unless something was wrong in the blood results. Muddy took it and thought she would get it filled if it stopped the kerplunks. She was relieved she didn't need open heart surgery or have cancer. "Thank ya'll," she said as she buttoned her blouse and the nurse helped her down from the table.

"You're welcome," the nurse said. The doctor had already gone out, either on to the next patient or out the back door to lunch.

Muddy drove through the Walgreen's pharmacy and told them she'd be back to pick it up and the clerk told her it would be about an hour. Muddy drove on to the Bistro, where Lily and Anthony were waiting at a table.

"Did everything go well?" Lily asked.

"Sure did. The prescription he gave me will keep those little heart episodes from occurring. I'll pick it up after lunch."

"That's great," said Lily.

"Is Kathy going to join us?"

"I don't think so," said Anthony.

"I was hoping she'd change her appointment and come anyway. You'll have to bring her to the house for supper one night."

"Who's Kathy?" Lily asked.

"She's a lady I've been seeing some," said Anthony.

"What?" Lily asked. "I hadn't heard this news."

"You know how he is," said Muddy. "Wouldn't tell you if he'd won the lottery."

"Good for you," said Lily.

"We met in class at the college, which is where she works," said Anthony.

"I'm proud of you finally going back to get a degree," said Muddy. "If I were a little younger, I'd go back and get one, too."

"You're going back to college?" Lily asked.

"Sure am, Lily. Best thing I've done for myself in a while." He turned to his mother: "Mama, you ought to think about it, too. After 65, it's fee."

"What if it's after 75? Is there some other kind of bonus added?"

They both laughed. "You really ought to think about it. Get out and meet some more people."

"I appreciate it, but I don't want to drive all the way over here to take classes. Besides, Mr. Stalvey is keeping me plenty busy."

"Velma's telling others ya'll went dancing last night and I already had a call."

"Well, that's not entirely true, and you know Velma well enough to know that. Mr. Stalvey occasionally likes to play Bingo out at the old school in Dixie. They do have a country band that plays some, and some of the older people dance. So, I went. No big deal, really, but it was nice to get out and do something. Of course, Velma was there and raised her eyebrows and spoke. I suspected she'd spread rumors. She always has. Some people never change, but you know, if the world didn't have stupid people, it might get pretty boring."

Lily and Anthony laughed and nodded. They all ordered salads and made small talk. They laughed about the gun shot, they all expressed good feelings about Hank Holloway, and they talked about Claude, how much they missed him and laughed at some of the things they remembered he'd done or said—his killing a rattlesnake that fell from a tree right next to him, his nearly burning the house down throwing gasoline on the fire when it had died down, his praying out loud in church and saying, "Lord, forgive them people in Washington for all this crazy shit." Muddy hadn't heard it in a while from the children and she hadn't heard it from anyone at the church in some time, but she knew no one had ever forgotten it. Of course, it had slipped out and Claude was embarrassed. He didn't use a lot of curse words, but that was one he kept on using. They talked about church on Sundays, her fried chicken and macaroni and cheese lunches afterwards, naps in the afternoons on the front porch. They talked about Disney World, beach trips, and yard work.

When there was a lull in conversation, Muddy said, "We've had a good life. I don't believe I would have changed a thing if I had a chance to do it over."

Epilogue

For all of us mothers and fathers who struggle to do the best we can and realize we can only live and control some of our own lives, not others'

Muddy lived on another five years, long enough to see Anthony finally graduate with his college degree, long enough to see both her grandsons graduate from high school, and long enough to have a good relationship with Fred Stalvey. She was happy to see Tom go to her alma mater in Tifton, study forestry like his daddy.

It was several weeks after Bingo and the first dance that Muddy and Fred actually spent the night together, and it was difficult for both of them to do, not the physical part, but the mixed emotions that went with it - the positive feelings of love combined with the deep feelings of loss and guilt. Nonetheless, they were discrete and proper as could be, and over time, Mr. Stalvey came to be appreciated and respected by Muddy's children, being invited to family gatherings, like Christmas day. He even got a matching bathrobe to one Muddy had been given by the grandchildren, but Muddy knew it was Lily who made the purchase, not her grandsons. They even established three scholarships at the college where Muddy had gone in memory of each of their spouses and in memory of Cassie Harris.

Muddy and Fred spent four years together, though they never moved in together or married, and Fred contracted colon cancer. Even after surgery, they thought they had it all, but it reappeared a few months later in his liver and spine. He didn't last long, and Muddy spent day and night with him, nursing him and even giving him pain medicine when the Hospice nurse couldn't be there. She knew he loved her and appreciated her, but he had always been in love with Charlene, just as she had Claude. Muddy had held his hands, singing sweetly the country gospel songs Fred loved, and when he took his last breath, he smiled, a tear rolling from one eye. Muddy knew he had crossed to Charlene, and she was happy for him, though she'd be alone again. She imagined Charlene standing on the edge of the river, waiving and thanking her for all the help.

Hank Holloway sent a Christmas letter, updating friends, relatives, and parishioners on the goings-on at the church in East Tennessee and the automobile repair shop, especially when they acquired a nearly rusted Nash, painted it, and mounted it on metal poles some forty feet off the ground, all as a form of advertising, which apparently worked as business nearly doubled that year. Holloway even came to Morven on another trip to Florida to visit for a few hours three years after his first. He'd even been called to testify when the Florida School for the Boys endured their final investigation which led to closure.

Todd and Shaneka became more involved their first year of college in Thomasville, and their sophomore year, Shaneka gave birth to a baby girl. There had been times in South Georgia, when they were together, and when Shaneka was pregnant and showing, that people had turned their heads in disgust, or made comments under their breath. On two different occasions, Todd and Shaneka almost ran into trouble. In one instance Muddy heard about, the two were shopping, and a couple of mean-looking redneck types called Todd a "nigger lover," at which he turned on his heels, and pulled his pistol. They ran off. In a different scenario, Todd and Shaneka were in the IGA picking up some chicken to grill, and two black men said something about Shaneka being a "honkey lovin' bitch," and again, Todd pulled the pistol and they slowly walked away like penguins, pants sagging. Muddy wasn't negative or judgmental about the relationship and felt the great grandchild they named after her and called "Muddy" was beautiful, but would have a tough row to hoe in South Georgia even all these years later after Civil Rights and integration. Muddy was also glad Todd had taken the pistol, had it officially registered to him, and had taken out a concealed weapons permit to protect him and Shaneka. Muddy felt that perhaps this, in some small way, had helped with the ancestral sins, if such was even possible, though they'd never learned the full story, at least that she was aware. She also thought that electing a black president would help racial relations, but she didn't know if it had. She hadn't voted for Obama because she didn't like his policies, but McCain just couldn't compete with a young, charismatic candidate and lost. While Todd and Shaneka hadn't gotten married, they did live together. Muddy felt like they were living in sin and not doing the baby Muddy justice in that arrangement and also felt like they should get involved in a church. She didn't preach it to them, however.

Timothy continued to practice law in Tifton, and he and Nancy were involved in the community. She noted how gray Timothy's hair had become, how he had lost muscle mass, and how he was aging faster in his face, in his eyes. She had encouraged him to slow, to enjoy life a bit more. He'd laugh at his mother when she encouraged it and had a massive heart attack in church one Sunday morning. After a few days in the hospital, he recovered and began to eat a bit healthier, as Muddy had taught him. Muddy was glad he'd recovered. She couldn't bear the thought of burying one of her own.

Anthony married Kathy shortly after his graduation. They lived together in his house, and when they have a chance, they take vacations all over the United States with seniors on a bus from Thomasville. They serve as guides and assistants to the retired minister and his wife who direct the trips. So far, they've seen the Grand Canyon, Niagara Falls, Mount Rushmore and Old Faithful. Their next trip will be to see the Redwood forests in Northern California. They even took Muddy to the mountains in the fall to see the leaves, and they visited the Holloway family. Muddy even saw the Nash Hank had put on a pole at his garage and she liked it.

Lily was the child Muddy had to spend the most time with in her final years. Lily and Sid didn't like Todd's relationship and felt people, their friends and their church, had treated them differently since that relationship. Lily had withdrawn some and Sid's work, his client base in forestry, had declined. This all served to bring them closer together, and Muddy and Lily had many conversations, working together to overcome obstacles life naturally unfolded in front of them to help them grow and blossom. Lily redid her bedroom after Muddy died and after the stitching was repaired, Lily now covers with the old quilt. Now, Lily rubs her feet underneath the cool cotton backing at night. She keeps little Muddy some while Todd and Shaneka eke out a living, working part time and trying to finish their degrees.

After Fred Stalvey died, Muddy got a housekeeper and helper. Maria had become her friend, coming in three days a week, and Muddy even learned a little Spanish; she enjoyed practicing when she went to the Mexican restaurant in Thomasville. Muddy later learned she was the grandmother of one of the migrant workers killed outside Tifton.

Muddy went home in 2013, dying peacefully in her sleep and crossing over to see Claude, her parents, Fred and Charlene, and many other friends and relatives who'd crossed before her. Maria came in one Monday morning and found Muddy still in bed. "Come on, Charlotte, it's time," the voice whispered, and Muddy reached for the angel's hand, and drifted up and out and crossed the cool waters to the shore where Claude stood surrounded by a soft, white light.

Maria called Timothy who then called Lily and Anthony, as she'd often been instructed to do. The service at the Methodist church was nice, and the church was full. Hank Holloway came to Morven and did a eulogy after the minister spoke. All of Muddy's favorites were played, and even Crazy Jenny came to pay her respects.

They were all sad to see Muddy go, and each year on her birthday, on holidays, on Mother's Day, they would remember her and cry because there will forever remain a hole in their hearts until they, too, drift too far, when the cycle of life will once again repeat itself until the river dries and the two shores come together.

Her children divided the belongings over time and put the house up for sale. They enjoyed going through the photos their mother had left for them, labeled, in shoeboxes, and they weren't sure what to do with the clippings through the years from all of the crimes and tragic events Muddy had kept. Lily decided to take them, read them, and later decided we are shaped and guided by events whether they touch us directly or not.

The house stayed on the market for six months before a young couple with two children from Hahira bought it. They trimmed the hedges low, cut the azaleas back, and tore down the barn out back, using the wood for a deck surrounding an above-ground pool and removing the swing and placing Adirondack chairs on the porch. Muddy wouldn't have approved the changes.

Acknowledgements

I can't begin to describe my appreciation to all the victims I have memorialized in these pages who inspired me, especially Mary Turner. I am also appreciative to the writers and singers of the song "Drifting Too Far From The Shore". I am appreciative of Erin Z. Bass, editor of *Deep South* magazine, for publishing what became the first chapter of *Drifting Too Far From The Shore*. I am eternally appreciative of my wife Michelle's patience for enduring iterations of chapter after chapter of my reading and editing aloud. I am appreciative to Holley Wood who assisted me with the redesign and technical edits of my website: www. nilesreddick.com to promote Drifting. For Pulitzer nominee and writer-friend Janice Daugharty's never ending support and encouragement, I am grateful. For my beloved Southern Georgia place, family, and friends who are always close in my thoughts, I remain blessed and inspired. For the readers and book clubs who tell me to keep writing, I am appreciative. For my editor in Paris, France, Laurel Zuckerman, I am humbled and honored you gave Muddy Rewis the chance to bring her story to life.

About the Author

Niles Reddick's collection *Road Kill Art and Other Oddities* was a finalist for an Eppie award; his novel *Lead Me Home* was a national finalist for a ForeWord Award and a finalist in the Georgia Author of the Year award in the fiction category. His work has appeared in anthologies: *Southern Voices in Every Direction* (Iris Press), *Unusual Circumstances* (Pocol Press), *Getting Old* (KY Story), and *Happy Holidays* (Kind of Hurricane Press). Author of over 50 short stories, Niles' work has appeared in multiple literary magazines and journals including *The Arkansas Review: a Journal of Delta Studies, Southern Reader, The Dead Mule School of Southern Literature, The Pomanok Review, Corner Club Press, Slice of Life, Deep South Magazine, Spelk, Faircloth Review, New Southerner, Sonder Literary Magazine, The Harpoon Review*, and many others. He works for the University of Memphis, Lambuth, in Jackson, Tennessee.

His website is www.nilesreddick.com